Striker

Second Leg

The Left winger delicately chipped the ball to Ben in the middle. Ben chested it down and turning with it struck the ball as it hit the ground. It came off his foot like a thunderbolt! The back of the net rippled and bulged, and the opposing goalkeeper stood there with his mouth open. One up! Brenton Boys were on a winning streak again.

Yet a few weeks earlier it hadn't looked as if they'd ever win anything again. When they heard they were losing their pitch they thought they might have to disband. But Brenton were fighters. Their supporters worked all hours to convert Donald Owen's meadow into a first-class pitch and organised a fête to buy the building materials for the clubhouse. Ben's father, an ex-England player, gave his time and expertise to train them. With all that support, they just had to win!

Ben Dyker, his father and Brenton Boys scored a great success with "Striker". All football enthusiasts will enjoy this exciting story based on the popular BBC 1 series.

STRIKER
SECOND LEG

Kenneth Cope

British Broadcasting Corporation

For Renny

Published by the
British Broadcasting Corporation
35 Marylebone High Street
London W1M 4AA

ISBN 0 563 17288 6
First published 1977
© Kenneth Cope 1977

Printed in England
by Hazell Watson & Viney Ltd,
Aylesbury, Bucks

By the same author: *Striker*

The second series of *Striker*, by Kenneth Cope, was first
shown on BBC 1 in November and December 1976, with
Kevin Moreton as Ben, Sylvia O'Donnell as Jacky,
Geoffrey Hinsliff as Mr Dyker and Jo Gladwin as Harry.
The series was directed by Colin Cant and produced
by Anna Home.

One

Ben Dyker pushed his plate away from him, he felt full and very happy. He glanced round the hall, his face flushed, his hair still plastered down over his ears from the shower after the Cup Final. He looked at the other members of the Brenton team, sticking their faces into the fruit salad and cream. Soggy had finished already, of course. Ben looked at the top table, where the Cup they had won that afternoon glittered proudly. His father was sitting next to Molly, Soggy's mother, they didn't seem to have much to say to each other. Ben smiled, he knew his father wasn't at his best at this sort of function. Mr Robson, Mark's dad, sat the other side of his father. The parents and helpers had decorated the hall with bunting in the team's colours, blue, red and white. Up in the rafters a huge net bulging with hundreds of blown-up balloons swung gently. Ben ricked his neck looking up at them. He rubbed his left shin, that right back of theirs took a few liberties with his studs, he thought. Ben felt someone's eyes on him, and looked down the table, it was Nicky. He pulled a face and Nicky laughed, then he heaved a sigh, patted his stomach and gingerly stretched his legs under the table. He noticed that old Harry was talking Mark, the team's Captain, to death . . .

"Do you know," Harry was saying, "I haven't half enjoyed this, it's just like a wedding, isn't it?"

"It would have been like a funeral if we hadn't won," said Bomber.

"Four three," said Cheddar. "What a game, I'm dead stiff!"

"You were dead stiff before we started," said Dolly. Everybody laughed, Cheddar was well known for his complaints and his ability to invent homework on a cold practice night.

Soggy shouted to Nicky. "Have they got to my winning goal yet?" The table groaned.

Nicky turned to Mark. "We've had it now you know, we'll never hear the last of Soggy's magical run." Just before the referee had blown his whistle, Soggy had scored the winning goal. Now his head was growing larger every minute.

"What got into you Soggy?" shouted Mark.

"I'm still sticking to my theory he was stung by a bee," said Nicky.

Soggy treated this with disdain. "I could see an individual effort was called for," he said loftily. "I could see you lot had nothing left and would be wiped out in extra time, so I did what I did."

"Thank God he was pointed in the right direction when he got the ball," said Nick.

Soggy shook his still swelling head. "And what does that mean?"

"Nothing," said Nick. "I just wanted to point out that you've scored more goals against us than any visiting forward." This was an exaggeration, but Soggy, with a dreadful back pass to the goalie, Wayne, had put the ball into their own net. This had put the other team, Southcombe, three up, and everyone had thought the Final and the Cup lost. But Brenton had fought like mad after Mr Dyker's roasting at half-time and pulled three back in the second half. There the matter stood until Soggy's magical run just before the full-time whistle.

"I've already explained about that," said Soggy. "That own goal was a misunderstanding."

"Yeah," said Bomber. "A misunderstanding between you and everyone else in the South of England."

Soggy's sister, Jacky, shouted down the table. "Are they getting at you Soggy?"

"No," said Soggy. He looked at Nicky, "Are you?"

"What! Get at our match winner, our little Sogg, not on your life!"

Jacky wasn't entirely satisfied with this and she glared at Nicky. "Let me know if they do, Sogg," she shouted. Then turning to Ben she asked him in a softer voice, "Would you like some more fruit salad Ben? I can get you some if you do."

Dolly jumped in very quickly. "I'd like some Jacky."

"You get your own."

Ben shook his head and smiled, "No thanks Jacky, I'm full up."

"I'd like some," said Nicky. "No cream though, just the fruit salad."

Mark joined in grinning. "I'll have some as well," he said.

Soggy, not understanding what was going on, said, "I wouldn't mind some more, our Jacky."

Jacky started to get angry at the boys. She had a crush on Ben and the other members of the team teased about it. She glared at Nicky, "I didn't ask you, 'Snazz Harry'."

Nicky put his arm round Dolly, nodded at Ben and said loudly, "He got extra ham as well, did you notice Dolly? *And* three slices of brown bread. I think it's disgusting!"

Dolly agreed with him, "Favouritism, that's what it is!"

Jacky looked daggers at Nicky. "You want to keep your remarks to yourself, Nicky Brown."

"Sorry," said Nicky, realising he'd gone too far.

"Yes, well," said Jacky.

"He said he was sorry, Jacky," said Soggy.

Jacky turned on him, her eyes flashing. "You shut up," she said.

Suddenly Mr Robson started to bang on the table. "Order, order now, lads. Settle down, come on. Settle down, please."

The boys turned their faces up to the top table. All their eyes were drawn to the Cup, its polished bowl reflecting their victory. A hush descended on the hall. Ben glanced round at all the friends he'd made in Brenton Football Club, and caught his father's eye. He was looking very stern, but he smiled when he nodded at Ben.

"Thank you, thank you, ladies and gentlemen," said Mr Robson. "Ladies and gentlemen, boys of Brenton Football team, parents, supporters." Mr Robson spread his arms. "I hope you have all enjoyed the humble supper we have been able to offer you tonight."

The hall exploded into a frenzy of noise. The boys went mad, stamped their feet, banged plates, shouted "Hear, hear." Bomber called out, "What supper?" and got his laugh. Someone was blowing a referee's whistle, while Jacky had the supporters' rattle and was nearly taking old Harry's head off with her twirling. Even the top table was wreathed in smiles. Mr Robson held his arms up until the noise subsided, then touched the rim of the Cup and cleared his throat.

"Looking at that makes me very proud," he said. "It's the first Cup in the history of Brenton. I never thought we would see it standing there on our annual dinner table. Well done lads!" The parents started to applaud. Mr Robson went on: "We shall arrange for every player to have the Cup for a week, to keep in his own home."

Dolly shouted out, "Don't let Soggy have it, he'll flog it."

Everybody laughed.

"It's my pleasant duty now to propose a vote of thanks to all the people behind the scenes, who have helped the Club during the season." Mr Robson glanced at his notes. "Firstly, Mrs Harris and her band of helpers, for laying on this supper, this evening." The ladies looking through the kitchen hatch blushed and disappeared as everybody turned and looked at them, then waved through the hatch to acknowledge the applause.

Mr Robson went on, "And Mr Harry Ainsworth for the care and marking out of the pitch." Harry glowed with self-importance as the team applauded . . . "And all the supporters," continued Mr Robson. "You, yourselves." There was sustained applause and this time Mr Robson had to sit down until the cheering stopped.

Old Harry, the team's groundsman, assistant coach, chief scout, and bottle washer, stood up. His face flushed with excitement, he had to shout for quiet. "There's somebody I'd like to propose a big 'thank you' for, Mr Robson," he said. He pointed to Jacky, "There's a little girl here who, every week, gets out these lads' jerseys spotless. She never grumbles, never moans . . ."

Dolly shouted, "She just gives you a back hander."

Harry nodded at the laughter, "Maybe, maybe, but for my money she's as good as gold. She's a good 'un, a little worker, she does all the fixtures as well." He turned to the lads. "I'm surprised none of you lads have seen fit to pay her any respects and all. Ladies and gentlemen, little Jacky, bless her." Harry started to applaud, and the rest of the room rose and clapped as well. Soggy stood on his chair and clapped the loudest. Bomber, never one to miss an opportunity, placed a dish of trifle on the seat behind him to give Soggy a welcome befitting his name, when he sat down again. Nicky stood up and waved his arms about to get a bit of quiet.

"Ladies and gentlemen," began Nicky, "helpers, supporters, fellow players and Soggy." The hall laughed, and then laughed even more when Soggy discovered what he'd sat in. Bomber was nearly choking.

Nicky waited for them to settle down. "The team has been aware of Jacky's hard efforts on our behalf," said Nick. "And we have all agreed to show our gratitude in a little presentation. We had planned to do it a little later on, but Harry has forced our hand as it were." Nicky looked at Harry – Harry didn't know where to put himself.

He polished his glasses furiously, breathing flames on to the lenses and flapping his clean handkerchief.

Mark stood up and leaned across the table. Soggy ducked because he thought Mark was going to thump him, but he was only handing Nicky a small package.

"Thank you Mark," said Nicky, very formally.

"Not at all Nick," said Mark straight-faced.

Nicky held up the package. At that moment Jacky would have liked the ground to swallow her up. Nicky Brown, of all people, she thought.

"On behalf of the team, Jacky, we would like you to accept this small gift." He handed the package to Jacky and everybody clapped her again. Her eyes opened wide as she saw what it was, then she held up the contents so everybody could see. It was a silver charm necklace with eleven little footballers hanging from it.

Jacky handed it to Nicky, and for a minute he thought she was giving it back to him. Then he realised what she wanted him to do. He fastened the necklace round her neck and smiled at her. Jacky kissed his cheek and the hall went wild. All the lads stamped and drummed on the table. Soggy leant into Dolly. "Eh," he said. "I didn't know about that!"

"Dead right you didn't," replied Dolly. "You owe us ninety pence."

"Why didn't anyone tell me?" said Soggy.

Dolly looked at him. "Are you any good at keeping secrets Sogg?"

Soggy shook his head, "No."

"Ninety pence, don't forget."

"How much?" Soggy sat there with his mouth open.

Mr Robson banged the table with a spoon to get the hall's attention again. He cleared his throat and so did all the team. Mr Robson smiled and nodded. "Now we come to the man who made it all possible." He gestured to Mr Dyker, who was looking more uncomfortable by the minute. "Without his help, without his patience in showing the boys skills they never thought they had; without him giving up so much of his own time, this –" Mr Robson pointed to the Cup – "would never have been ours. Ladies and gentlemen, Mr Dyker . . ."

If there had been noise before, it was a whisper compared with what happened next. Mr Dyker got to his feet, a nervous smile on his face, and stood there as the hall erupted again. The team stood to a man, applauding him. Soggy kept checking his chair in case Bomber had left anything on it.

Mr Dyker looked at Ben, who was cheering with the rest. Slowly the applause died and the hall reseated itself. Mr Dyker shook his head, "I'm not very good at this," he said.

Dolly called: "Chest it down lad, come on, run on, run on!"

Mark joined in: "Effort lads! Effort! Come on, let's see some style!"

Bomber shouted: "Push! Push! Take the defender with you. Go wide, go wide."

Mr Dyker nodded at them. "I'm glad to see some of you listen."

"I always do, Mr Dyker," shouted Soggy.

Mr Dyker waved at him. "You played a blinder, Soggy."

"When he got the ends sorted out," shouted Nicky. Everyone laughed at the expression on Soggy's face.

"I won't say much," continued Mr Dyker. "You've taken me and Ben in. We're very grateful, we're very happy here. You say I've done a lot for you, I'd like to say you've done twice as much for us. You're nice people . . . thank you, all of you." Mr Dyker sat down.

The cheering went on and on. A lot of boys would be hoarse on the next day.

Mr Robson held up his hands for silence. Slowly the hall went quiet. He seemed to be in some sort of difficulty. He got out some papers and placed them in front of him. He looked about, there was a very long pause. Finally Mr Robson spoke, very quietly. The hall seemed to sense that something was wrong.

"I would . . . I would . . ." Mr Robson began again. "I would give anything not to have to do what . . . I wish . . . Ladies and gentlemen," he pointed to a thin man sitting at the end of the top table. "Mr Eckersley, who you all know is our senior Council Member, has very kindly agreed to attend our dinner tonight, and to explain something which, I'm afraid, will be a terrible shock to most of you."

Mark went cold, he could tell from the way his father spoke that something very serious had happened.

Mr Eckersley stood up. "Ladies and gentlemen," he began, "this is not easy, so please bear with me. Fallowfield, as you all know, houses the men's football pitch and our victorious boys . . ." He was drowned by shouts of, "The men are rubbish!" "Soggy could play them on his own," and so on. When the shouts died away he continued: "Mr Gilbert, who owned the field as you all know, died last year."

Soggy whispered to Dolly. "Eh, is that why we had to wear those black armbands against Molton?"

"What did you think they were for?" asked Dolly.

"No idea."

Dolly looked at him in disgust.

"Mr Gilbert had loved football all his life. He loved this town. He loved coming to these dinners." Mr Eckersley looked round the room. "He charged us nothing at all for the use of Fallowfield, just a written undertaking to keep it mown, tidy, and safe and free for children." Mr Eckersley paused again. "I think each of us in this room has taken advantage of Mr Gilbert's generosity at one time or another. I'm afraid Fallowfield has had to be sold to afford Mr Gilbert the luxury of dying. Heavy death duties have fallen on his family. I'm sorry to tell you that houses are going to be built on Fallowfield. The contractors are starting next week." Mr Eckersley waved his arms about in a helpless way and continued: "We held them off as long as possible. There is nothing, nothing at all, we can do." He sat down. The hall buzzed, everyone was talking at once.

Soggy asked Harry, "Does that mean we lose our pitch?"

"I'm afraid it does lad, I'm afraid it does."

"Where are we going to play then?"

It was Nicky who answered Soggy. "I think we've all just retired from football."

"I don't understand," said Mark. "Dad didn't say anything to me."

Nicky was choked. "We went out with a bang though, didn't we?"

Mark nodded. "We were just coming good."

Soggy shouted, "Why can't we play all our matches away?"

"You have to have a home pitch to qualify for the League, you daft nit," said Nicky.

"Oh," said Soggy. He looked over to Jacky, and saw that tears were streaming down her face. "What's the matter, our Jacky?" he shouted.

"Nothing," she sniffed, her shoulders heaving.

"You're crying!" said Soggy.

Jacky shook her head, her long hair hiding her face. "No, I'm not."

"Yes you are."

"I'm not."

"She is, isn't she, look at her!" Soggy persisted.

"Soggy!" shouted Ben.

"What?"

"Shut up!"

"Right Ben, right," said Soggy, stealing another look at Jacky. She had her head down and was studying the necklace intently.

On the top table Mr Dyker looked as though he'd been hit on the head. Molly had to speak to him twice before he responded. "I said I wanted to thank you for taking such an interest in Crispin."

"Who?" asked Mr Dyker.

"Soggy," said Molly with a smile.

"Oh, yes."

"I'm his mother."

"How do you do," said Mr Dyker.

Molly smiled, "You've done wonders with him."

"He's a steady player, he's got good reactions."

"He likes you an awful lot. He's always talking about you."

"He's very keen," said Mr Dyker.

"What will you do now they've taken the pitch away from you?"

Mr Dyker stared straight ahead. "You can't play football without a pitch, can you?"

"It's such a shame," said Molly. "Look at all their faces!"

Mr Dyker glanced down the hall. The boys were all looking towards the top table, hoping for a miracle, hoping for someone to stand up and say it was only a joke. Mr Dyker reached out and ran his finger round the rim of the Cup.

"It's funny, isn't it?" he said, almost to himself. "You get something, hold it in your hand, start to build, and just as you're saying it's all right, this time it's all right –" he pushed the cup away – "someone takes it all away from you." He shook his head.

Molly looked at him. "You mustn't let it make you bitter," she said.

Mr Dyker just nodded in reply, then stood up, shook hands with Mr Robson, collected Ben and left the hall.

Two

Mr Dyker strode round the caravan site picking up their gear and packing it away. Ben followed him miserably. They had been up very early and Ben had made breakfast while his father shaved.

Mr Dyker hadn't spoken much, just told Ben what to do, pick this up, pack that. When Ben asked him anything he snapped his head off. It's just like old times thought Ben. Us moving on, Dad mad as hell, everything falling to bits round us. Ben fought back the choking feeling at the back of his throat. His eyes started to fill with tears. He bent to pick up an old bowl of water, placed under the caravan for Harry's dog, Bob.

"What shall I do with this, Dad?" he asked, turning away so that his father couldn't see his face.

"Throw it over the hedge," snapped his father.

"I'll leave it for Harry," said Ben.

"Why did you ask me then?" shouted Mr Dyker.

Ben looked at his father, hopping about with his bad leg, his face red and sweaty with the effort of clearing up.

He felt Ben's eyes on him and turned, then saw Ben's miserable face. Mr Dyker softened and went over to put his arm on Ben's shoulder.

"Don't you think I should say goodbye to them all, Dad?"

Mr Dyker shook his head. "No point son, no point."

"We can't just go," said Ben.

Mr Dyker ruffled Ben's hair. "Believe me Ben, it's better this way. There's nothing here for us now."

Ben sniffed, "There's nothing for us anywhere."

Mr Dyker put his hand under Ben's chin and gently raised his head. "When you're old enough to go your own way, you can. Until then, you stick with me, right?"

Ben bit his lip. "I don't want to go my own way, Dad. I just want to . . ." He broke off and leaned against the side of the caravan.

"Look Ben, we thought this might be a place to settle, yes? It had possibilities, right?"

Ben nodded, "You seemed happier here, Dad."

"Yes, well, it's exploded in our faces, hasn't it? It always does Ben, learn that simple fact and you'll never get trodden on."

"I thought you liked it here," said Ben.

"I did Ben, I did. I made a mistake, I let myself get carried away. I let my guard down. I felt at home here. It's been a mistake Ben, believe me."

Ben shook his head. "There must be somewhere where we could get things to go right."

Mr Dyker patted him on the shoulder and closed and locked the caravan door. "We'll find it Ben, wherever it is, we'll find it. Come on." He opened the landrover passenger door for Ben. "Come on Ben, get in, lets be off."

"What about your job at the garage, Dad?"

"I told them I wouldn't be coming back."

Ben looked across the site to the pitch in the distance. Two little kids were kicking in the goal. Ben looked at his father. "Of all the places we've been, I think this . . ." Ben dropped his head.

"Come on son," said Mr Dyker gently. "In you get." He helped Ben into the landrover, then went round and got in the driving seat. The engine coughed and spluttered into life. Mr Dyker revved it up, the cab shuddered and vibrated. Ben stared out of the window. Mr Dyker throttled back, looked across at Ben, and let the gear in. They both jumped as someone banged the side of the landrover.

It was Harry. He leaned into the cab. "Eh, you two, you're not sloping off without saying goodbye, are you?"

"Hello, Harry," shouted Mr Dyker.

Harry shook his fist at them. "Don't friends mean anything to you two then?" he shouted.

Mr Dyker let the engine idle. "Sorry Harry, it seemed the best way, no fuss, no bother."

Harry pulled a face, "That's nice, that is," he said, "you owe me half a bitter."

Mr Dyker smiled, "Harry you're unique, you're on your own. Goodbye old son." He held his hand out to Harry. "Wrap up well in the winter now, do you hear?"

The two men shook hands. Harry leaned across Mr Dyker and

shook Ben's hand. "We've seen some sights, haven't we Ben?"

Ben nodded, tears nearly starting again. Mr Dyker revved up.

"Mind you," shouted Harry, "there's no need to go now you know."

"What?" shouted Mr Dyker.

"I said, there's no need to go. We've had an offer."

"What?" shouted Mr Dyker again.

"An offer," yelled Harry.

Mr Dyker reached down and turned the ignition key and the engine stopped. "What are you on about?" he said.

Harry's eyes were twinkling. "We've got a pitch! Well, sort of a pitch."

"Where? Where?" asked Ben.

Harry took his time. "Donald Owen says we can have his north field. He said as long as we can drain it and level it."

Ben's face lit up. "Dad!" he shouted.

"Harry, look at me," said Mr Dyker. "Tell me honestly, is there a chance we could get it ready in time?"

Old Harry dropped his eyes. "It will take a lot of hard work."

Mr Dyker smiled kindly at him. "It's not on, is it Harry?"

"It's a chance. It's a chance." Harry blustered.

Mr Dyker patted Harry's shoulder and switched on the engine again. "Nice try Harry," he shouted. "Take care of yourself."

Mr Dyker let the gear in, and the landrover, with the caravan behind, lurched away. Harry stood there, Bob sniffing round his heels, watching them drive into the distance. An old woman walked past in front of Harry. He shouted to her. "He used to play for England, you know!"

"What?" she called.

"Him, in the landrover, he used to play for England."

"Did he?"

"Aye," said Harry, with pride.

"That's nice," replied the woman, and went to collect the children who were kicking about on the pitch.

Harry looked round the deserted site and shook his head. "Come on Bob, I'll race you to the bench." Bob just wagged his tail.

On the dual carriageway, Mr Dyker put his foot down. The ancient landrover whined in protest as he coaxed extra speed out of her. The caravan let Mr Dyker know, through the steering, what a drag it was. It swayed gently, left and right. Ben watched the trees lining the road flash past. He squinted his eyes so that they became a continuous blur. Ben had not moved since they had set off. He was still in the same slumped position.

His father sensed his misery and tried to cheer him up. "We'll drive for a while, then have some lunch. A proper one, bloody tablecloths and all, what do you say Ben?"

Ben was biting his bottom lip. He gave a short nod.

"I'm fed up with transport cafés and sandwiches, aren't you, little 'un?"

Ben had to make a big effort. "Anything you say, Dad." His voice broke slightly. Mr Dyker looked across at him. He sighed and drove harder.

"Don't worry," said Mr Dyker, changing lanes and overtaking a milk tanker. "We'll get sorted out, Ben. I'll get a job in town." He pounded the steering wheel. "We'll sell this lot. Maybe we could get a little flat together. You'd like that, wouldn't you Ben? Get you in a regular school, stop this charging about the country, flitting from place to place." Mr Dyker leaned forward in his seat to overtake a Morris saloon. After he was safely past, he went on: "Your Mam would kill me if she was alive, mucking you about the way I have. Not giving you a settled place."

At the mention of his mother, Ben lost all the control he had, tears ran unchecked down his cheeks. His mother had been killed in a car crash, eight years ago. She had had to go out to work when his father had been unable to move because of his leg injury. Ben and his father used to wait up for her after her long trips round the country to deliver samples. Mr Dyker told her, on the telephone, to stay overnight, but she said she had to be home for Mr Dyker's birthday. They had waited and waited until the policeman came. She had fallen asleep on the motorway and driven into a bridge. Ben still had dreams about it. He remembered the policeman standing there, slowly taking his helmet off. Asking was there a close relative nearby, before he said anything. And after he'd told them, he gave Ben a butterscotch, wrapped in paper, and said, don't worry son. Ben had kept the sweet for years. As long as he didn't unwrap it and eat it, his Mam would come back. It was ages before he threw it away.

Mr Dyker was still talking to him. "You know Ben," he said, "that place has been good for us. I've stopped snapping your head off. I enjoyed training those kids, I really did. Turned me on to football again." Mr Dyker wrestled with the wheel, as he changed gear to approach a roundabout. "Eh, Ben," he shouted above the revs. "We might get a holiday in this year. A proper one, what do you say?"

Ben couldn't answer him.

"We could go abroad, Spain or somewhere, what do you say?" As he went into the roundabout Mr Dyker looked across at Ben and saw the wet miserable face. Ben started to sob. "Eh, eh," said Mr Dyker, and drove hard right round the roundabout. The following cars hooted and drivers shouted as the caravan dipped and swayed in front of them. Mr Dyker pulled to a halt in the slip road.

"Why didn't you give a signal?" shouted a red-haired driver.

Mr Dyker obliged him with one there and then and turned to Ben and put his arms round him. Ben sobbed . . . they stayed like that for a while. Mr Dyker said quietly, "It's a long time since I did this."

Ben fought to control himself. "I'm sorry, Dad," he said.

Mr Dyker shook his head. "You cry it out son, go on."

"I won't be long now," said Ben bravely.

"Take as long as you like, son, you take your time."

Mr Dyker got a tissue from the glove compartment and offered it to Ben. "Do you think I'm hard on you, Ben?" he asked.

Ben sniffed away, mopping up. "You used to be," he said, "but I think that was Mam going, you know."

"Aye," said his Father. "I wonder what she'd do about all this, eh?"

Ben was feeling a little better. "She'd never let anybody get her down."

They sat in silence for a while. Mr Dyker was looking ahead, through the windscreen, ruffling Ben's hair. "She was a fighter, your Mam. Stood up to everybody."

Ben looked at him. "She'd laugh at us here, wouldn't she . . . me crying."

"She would that," agreed Mr Dyker. "She would that." Mr Dyker watched the speeding traffic for a little while, then he seemed to make his mind up. He turned to Ben, who was on his fifth tissue. "Shall we give it another try then? Shall we have a look at Harry's field?"

Ben looked into his father's eyes to see if he meant it. "We haven't got much time to get it ready."

Mr Dyker hugged him. "What do you say?" he shouted.

"It's up to you, Dad," said Ben, his face breaking into a smile this time.

Mr Dyker pressed his fist down on the horn and blew a long blast. "Come on," he shouted, "let's give it a go."

Ben laughed at the startled expressions of the motorists driving past.

"We'll give it a go," repeated Mr Dyker, and started the engine.

"You'll be able to get your job back, Dad," babbled Ben. "And Harry's no fool, if he thinks we can make a pitch out of it, it must have a chance. You don't have to show the League the pitch before the season. You just have to enter on the form where it is . . . oh, Dad, Dad," shouted Ben.

"OK son, OK, we'll see, we'll see," said Mr Dyker and lurched into a gap between a lorry and a van. The van driver objected, but Ben gave him a brilliant smile.

 Harry was dozing on the bench. Bob was yelping gently at his feet, asleep. Both of them were chasing memories. Harry was in his favourite stand position at Goodison Park, watching Everton show off Dixie Dean and his magical skills. Bob was chasing a rabbit, which kept getting bigger and turning on him as he was about to pounce. His legs quivered and he snarled gently, then yelped with fear. Harry was now watching Mr Dyker play, scoring the same goal, time after time, and seeing him fall and being clapped to the tunnel strapped on to a stretcher. The offending Birmingham player walked with him until Mr Dyker patted his arm and shook his hand and gestured to him to get back on the pitch. The crowd rose to see him down the tunnel.

Someone blew a car horn and Harry stirred slightly. They blew it again. Hooligans, thought Harry, bringing horns and trumpets to football matches. The horn got louder and Harry woke up. He could see the landrover across the pitch, and Ben waving madly. Harry jumped up, treading on Bob, who yelped for real, then Harry started to run towards Ben and Mr Dyker, with Bob snapping at his heels in excitement. Harry tried to give him a running kick but stumbled instead. "Give over, you stupid animal, give over," shouted Harry.

Ben laughed his head off. Harry came gasping up. "What kept you? What kept you? I knew you'd be back. I knew you'd be back!"

"Me Dad wants to have a look at the field," said Ben very excited.

"Does he now," said Harry. "Well, we'll have to arrange that for him, won't we?" Harry looked at Mr Dyker, his eyes twinkling. "I'll have that half a bitter off you now."

"It'll be a pleasure Harry, any time."

"Where's the field Harry, where is it?" asked Ben, dancing with excitement.

"Keep calm lad, you're like a grasshopper in a frying pan."

Mr Dyker unlocked the tow bar and moved the caravan onto a slight rise in the ground. He blocked the wheels and climbed into the landrover. "Come on you two, let's have a look at this field then."

"It's not far," said Harry, climbing in. Bob jumped in as well, and sat on the front seat with them. As the landrover moved off, Harry gave Mr Dyker directions. "You turn left out of here and keep going to the T junction." Mr Dyker worked his way through the gears and followed the route described by Harry. "Left! I said left!"

"I am going left, you daft thing," shouted Mr Dyker. "I have to swing right to get the lock on."

"Oh," said Harry. "Just as long as you know."

Bob started to lick Mr Dyker's ear. "Does he have to do that?" he asked.

"He thinks you're upset," replied Harry.

"I will be in a minute, if he doesn't stop."

Ben laughed, "Watch he doesn't start chewing, Dad."

"Where do I go now?" asked Mr Dyker.

"Oh, left again here," said Harry. "Mind the traffic though, watch how you come out, it's very busy."

Mr Dyker raised his eyes to heaven. "What with your dog licking my ears and you telling me how to drive . . ."

Harry said quickly, "It's about fifty yards down this road, boss."

They had turned into a small lane, with tall hedges on each side. A pheasant broke cover and flew across the bonnet. Bob barked and jumped about. Mr Dyker turned to Ben. "He's a good house dog,

·isn't he, frightening the birdies." Mr Dyker drove slowly down the lane. Harry's "fifty yards" became three hundred before he said, "There it is, that white gate."

Ben had been trying to see over the hedge, but it was too tall. As Mr Dyker parked in the gateway, Ben could at last see the field. His heart sank, it looked very uneven. They all jumped out. "There's a dirty great bull in it," shouted Ben.

"Well," said Harry, "he plays midfield right off."

"Can we go in?" asked Mr Dyker.

"Of course you can," said Harry, "go on."

"Aren't you coming with us?" asked Mr Dyker.

Harry was keeping a wary eye on the bull. "What do I know about pitches?" he asked.

"About as much as I know about bulls," said Mr Dyker. The bull turned and so did Mr Dyker, scorn on his face. "Honestly, Ben, it's a cow!"

"Well," replied Ben, "it had its back to me."

Harry was very brave now. "Let's go and have a look then, you two," he said, marching boldly into the field.

The cow raised its head and looked at them. Mr Dyker shut the gate and followed Ben and Harry into the centre of the huge field, and looked about him. Not bad, not bad he thought. "There's room for a pitch and plenty else besides, even if its not quite level."

"What are we going to do about that, boss?" Harry pointed to a large tree trunk lying in the middle of the field.

"Have it carted away," shouted Mr Dyker.

Ben started to run round the outside edge of the field. Mr Dyker watched him.

"You could pitch your caravan at this end, near those trees," said Harry. "There's a pond down there," and he pointed to the other end of the field.

Mr Dyker grunted. "We'll have to fill it in, won't we?" He shouted to Ben who was still running. "What's it like son?"

Ben danced along his imaginary touchline, arms high above his head. "It's great, Dad, great." Ben veered to the landrover and reached inside the cab. He produced the practice ball and booted it to his father.

Mr Dyker cursed as he hopped about to trap it dead. "I'll kill him," he said to Harry.

"What?"

"He's always kicking the ball on to my bad side, to make me work my leg."

Harry looked at him fondly. "That lad of yours is something special, do you know that?"

Mr Dyker looked at Harry for a little while, his eyes squinting against the sun. "I'm just beginning to realise that Harry."

"Good," said Harry, "there's hope for you yet."

Mr Dyker laughed and chipped the ball to him. Harry set off with it, down the field, with Bob barking his head off at him.

Mr Dyker laughed. Harry shot the ball hard at Ben. He took it on his chest and turned and dummied as it hit the floor. Bob, chasing in, went the wrong way, confused. Ben lazily lifted the ball and right-footed it to his father. Mr Dyker stood there as the ball hung in the air. He bent forward ever so slightly and caught the ball with his head and flicked it up. It bounced there again and again. Bob was leaping higher and higher to get it. Mr Dyker caught Bob on one of his big leaps and held him in his arms. The dog looked sheepish and very embarrassed. He licked Mr Dyker on the nose. Ben laughed, "Eh, Dad," he pointed, "you can have Harry, the cow and Bob, five minutes each way. I'll take you all on."

"Don't you be so cocky," shouted Mr Dyker. "Come on, we've got work to do." They all clambered back into the landrover. The cow gave a low moo. Harry stuck his head out of the window and mooed back.

It started to move quickly towards them. Harry panicked. "Eh, boss, get a move on, he's after me."

Ben laughed as they roared off with Harry looking over his shoulder at the black and white cow. He turned into the cab, "Put that cow in the right colours and he'll do fine, he's got a fine turn of speed."

Ben looked at his father. "It's a good pitch, isn't it, Dad?"

"Aye," said Mr Dyker. "It's got the makings of one."

"Those trees at that side would give good shelter," said Harry. "We can put the Clubhouse there."

Mr Dyker grunted, "Don't get carried away you two. We need a lot of men, working every evening until the season starts, to get it into shape."

"Where are we going now, Dad?"

"To see Mr Robson," Mr Dyker said.

"To get your job back?"

"That and a few other things."

Ben pulled a face to Harry. "He's Chairman of Brenton Football Club, isn't he?" asked Harry.

A light began to dawn on Ben's face. "Oh, I see."

"Without help, we haven't got a chance," said Mr Dyker.

A large lorry sounded its horn angrily, as Mr Dyker took the bend too sharply. They missed each other, just.

Harry nodded, "Without you keeping your eyes on the road, we haven't got a chance either."

There was silence in the cab for a while, then they all started to laugh. Bob barked and set them off even more.

Ben was looking out of the side window and saw a backside he recognised. It was Soggy, pedalling away like mad. Mark and Nicky were with him, they had their fishing gear. My Dyker stopped ahead of them. Ben leaned out of the cab as they cycled up. "Put your bikes on the back and get in," shouted Ben.

"Why? Where are we going?" yelled Soggy.

"Never mind asking questions, Soggy, come on."

The boys slung their bikes over the tailboard and climbed in.

"We're going fishing," shouted Soggy.

"So are we," replied Mr Dyker. "For some help!"

The landrover went on through the outskirts of Brenton. The boys waved at people they knew. Ben told them the news about the new pitch, and they all got very excited. Mr Robson's garage loomed up in the distance and Mr Dyker sounded the horn as he turned into the forecourt.

Mr Robson came running out of his little office as the landrover emptied its passengers. He turned to Mark, "I thought you were going fishing?"

Mark grinned, "I got stopped."

"What do you mean?"

Mr Dyker said, "Perhaps I'd better explain."

Mr Robson looked at him. "I thought you were sick this morning, not coming in you know."

"I'd like to explain about that as well," said Mr Dyker. "Is my job still open?"

"Of course it is," said Mr Robson. "Will someone please tell me what's going on?"

Everybody started to talk at once. A customer came up to the pumps and had to serve himself. Too late, Soggy offered to wipe his windscreen, but the man just looked at him, disgusted. Mr Robson took the money and pondered on the idea of Donald Owen's field, which Mr Dyker had finally been able to tell him about. Mr Robson spoke to all of them. "Listen," he said, "we'll get some invitations printed on my copier."

"Invitations?" asked Harry.

"Yes, Harry, invitations to an extra special meeting, tonight, of the Committee and Supporters of the Club. Have you lads got your bikes?"

"Yes!" they chorused.

"Well, round up the rest of the team, we need delivery men to reach everybody by tonight. Off you go, go on. Back here in thirty minutes. Mr Dyker and I will compose something to prise them from their television sets."

The lads got their bikes and raced away. The watching group could hear them as they pedalled into the distance.

"I'll get Bomber, Cheddar and Ian," shouted Soggy.

"I'll get Dolly and Niggle," shouted Nicky.

"I'll get Adrian and Brent," shouted Mark.

Mr Dyker shouted after them. "Don't forget Jacky!"

Soggy stuck his hand up and wobbled dangerously; recovered and rode on.

Mr Dyker, Harry, Ben and Mr Robson crowded into the tiny office to sort out the invitation letter. Mr Dyker, irritated by the customers, broke off to serve petrol from time to time, but was soon back in the office helping out.

Three

Mr Robson stood on the rostrum of the Village Hall, behind the green baize card table, his brown, highly polished shoes twinkling. He looked very smart and spruced up. He was waiting for a few latecomers to arrive; most of the parents were already there. The boys had worked like demons to reach everybody in time and a lot of the audience were still in their working clothes. A few of the men looked grumpy and as though they needed their teas. Mr Robson decided to start the meeting.

"Ladies and gentlemen, thank you for turning up at such short notice. It is a matter of great urgency."

"What is it?" a man shouted from the back. "Bloody motorway coming through again, or something?"

"No," said Mr Robson. "It's the boys' football team. I think most of you were at the football dinner and heard Mr Eckersley explain about the boys losing their pitch. Well, I expect a lot of you saw Mr Dyker and Ben leave the hall . . ." he paused. "They left Brenton as well this morning, and were going for good, but they came back. They came back with a proposition."

"What?" shouted the man again.

"A proposition to turn Donald Owen's north field into a new pitch for the boys."

"He grows wheat on that field," shouted Stan Baker, Dolly's father.

Mr Robson shook his head, "Not any more. He's given it to the Club."

"What do you want us to do?" asked Brian Woodgate. He was Niggle's father, and looked exactly like him.

Mr Robson looked at them all. "I want you to give me your muscle, your time, your patience, your goodwill, and help us to give the boys a pitch nobody can ever take away from them again. It's as simple as that."

24

The hall was still, there was silence, then Mrs Baker said in a loud clear voice: "I think that is very nice of Mr Owen. Count me in, Mr Robson, and my husband."

"Thank you Ann," said Mr Robson, and went on. "I know you are all busy and what I'm asking you to do is probably impossible. It will mean an awful lot of very hard work to get the pitch ready for the start of the season. We've got the loan of all the equipment from Mr Owen's farm, tractors and earth movers, on evenings and Sundays, but we need muscle to operate them. What do you say?"

Adrian's father shouted, "What about goal posts?"

"We can salvage those, and the nets before they pull the Clubhouse down," said Mr Robson.

"I'm on," shouted Bomber's father from the back.

"And me," called out Nicky's father. "I've always wanted to drive a tractor."

Mr Robson smiled at him. "A lot of holes need filling in. We'll have to shift a lot of earth."

A thin little man, in the front row, turned to his wife and said. "It'll be just like having an allotment again, won't it!"

"You're not going to grow lettuces on it, are you? It's for the boys," she said.

Mrs Baker shouted: "Eh, watch him, Mr Robson, he'll be planting potatoes on it." The hall laughed.

"When do we start?" shouted Adrian's father.

Mr Robson nodded his thanks to him. "Hands up all those who want to sign on."

All the hands went up. One man's hand was forced up by his wife. "Go on," she said, "you and your telly. It's about time you did something for the kids."

"All right, all right," he muttered. "I've got my hand up, haven't I?"

"Just see you don't leave the room then," she replied.

Outside, listening and occasionally peering in the open window, were Mark, Soggy, Dolly, Niggle and Ben. Mr Dyker was standing a little way off, leaning against the bonnet of the landrover, waiting for the reaction from the crowd inside the hall. He looked across at Ben, who was biting his fingernails. Mr Dyker started to bite his as well, then stopped and walked round the vehicle instead.

Inside the hall, Mr Robson held up both his hands and brought the babble of voices to a stop. "So it's all settled," he said. "We're going to give our boys a pitch to be proud of."

Mr Baker shouted out. "You can't let League Champions and Cup winners go begging, can you?"

"No you certainly can't," replied Mr Robson. "And that brings me to my next point." He looked around the room. "We'll have to raise money to buy turf and seed, also lime. Materials for the dressing rooms and, if we are going to be a Club with any respect, we should have a small stand."

The man at the back who hadn't said a word yet, suddenly spoke up. "Will there be a bar?" he asked.

His wife jumped in: "There he goes, ask him to build a pub and he'll be with you day and night, no problem."

Her husband turned to her. "I was only asking the gentleman did he foresee a bar in his plans."

She rounded on him. "Just you listen," she said. "Stop looking at your watch, the pubs won't close for hours yet. I'll foresee that you get there on time."

The audience laughed and the man muttered away.

Mr Woodgate stood up. "I've got an idea. Why don't we nick all the stuff we need for the dressing rooms from the builders who are putting up the houses on the old pitch?"

"They're using yellow brick," said Mr Baker. "I've seen them dumping loads on the site."

"We'll change the Club's colours," said Mr Woodgate, with a smile.

Mr Robson jumped in before this got out of hand. "I think we should steer clear of anything in that line. I was thinking more of collections at doors, charity shows, a fête, raffles, you know, things like that."

Mr Woodgate chimed in again. "We can have those as well."

"Just let Mr Robson get on with it, will you, please!" said Mr Baker, heavily.

Mr Woodgate's neck went crimson, he clenched his fists, and shuffled his feet about. "Are you looking for trouble?" he threatened.

"Gentlemen . . . Gentlemen," pleaded Mr Robson. "Please keep calm, I beg you. Nothing will be sorted out if we carry on like this."

Mr Baker turned to the rest of them. "I ask you," he said,

"stealing yellow brick and building a mile away with it! The man's daft."

"He meant well," said Mr Robson.

"He meant to get us nicked."

Mr Woodgate stood up, "Now look here . . ."

Outside, Soggy nearly fell off the window ledge. "Great!" he told the others, "there's going to be a barney."

"What do you mean?" asked Mark, holding Soggy in position.

"Niggle's dad is having a go at Dolly's dad."

"No contest," said Niggle.

Dolly turned on him, "What do you mean, no contest? My dad would win hands down."

"Rubbish!" shouted Niggle.

"He would," yelled Dolly.

"No chance, no chance, I'm telling you," countered Niggle.

"Now look here . . ." said Dolly.

And it looked as though the two lads were nearly through the ritual to a punch-up, when Ben intervened. "Shut up you two, you're worse than your dads."

"He started it!" said Niggle and Dolly together.

Ben shook his head. "Soggy started it," he said.

They all looked at Soggy peeping into the hall. Mark was doing sterling service underneath, considering Soggy's weight. Ben looked up at him, "What's happening now, Soggy?"

"Dolly's dad's taken all his clothes off and the rest are drawing him, like we do in art."

"Watch it, big head," said Dolly.

"Don't you start on me," said Soggy. "If it wasn't for me, you would have lost your final."

"Oh, no," said Dolly, "he's off again!"

Soggy looked down at them all and started once more on his action replay. "I beat one feller," he said, eyes going bright with the memory. "I beat another feller, kicked their flash centre forward for kicking me, raced on with the ball, beat their left back, and with a beautiful body swerve, made the goalie go the wrong way; then and only then, did I hammer it into the back of the net."

"Eighty-seven times," said Dolly very loudly.

"Pardon?" said Soggy.

"I've heard that story eighty-seven times."

"I'd love to see a replay of it," said Soggy, wistfully.

"We'll try and lay it on for you," said Ben.

"And you can bore us through it." Mark just had to put Soggy down. He then looked through the open window.

"What's happening?" asked Niggle.

"I think the meeting is drawing to a close," said Mark.

"See, thick heads," crowed Soggy. "I told you they were drawing in there."

The others fell on Soggy. Some jokes just should not be allowed.

Mr Dyker heard footsteps coming up the red cinder path, and turned to see Harry, Bob in tow, of course. "How's it going?" asked Harry.

Mr Dyker showed Harry his crossed fingers. "Looks favourable, looks favourable," he grinned. "We're just waiting to hear." They both listened as long and sustained applause was heard from the hall.

Soggy was on his feet now and started to bow, pretending it was for him. The others jumped on him again. Harry gazed at them fondly, "They've got a lot of spirit, those lads," he said.

"Aye, Harry," said Mr Dyker, "but they're cheeky with it, I've got to watch them. Get them right and they'll give you the lot."

"Aye."

The front door of the hall opened and the parents and supporters came out, blinking in the sunshine, talking to each other. Mr Robson came out looking drained, and not so spruce as he had started. He hurried over to Mr Dyker and Harry. "Here it comes," said Harry. "We'll soon know, one way or the other."

As Mr Robson approached his face fell into a big grin. He looked at them both, then opened his arms to them. "Gentlemen, it's on! They've pledged to give us a pitch in time to qualify for the County League."

All the boys had followed Mr Robson, gathering round behind him. As they heard what he had to say, they gave a big cheer and started to jump up and down. Mr Dyker gave Ben a hug, and everyone went mad for a while. Mr Dyker calmed them down, "All right, all right, you lads, training in the new field tomorrow. We've got Cups to win!" This started them all off again, cheering and shouting.

Molly had come running up and she had to shout at the top of her voice to get any attention. The boys finally stopped their racket, and

Molly managed to make herself heard. "Soggy, have you seen our Jacky?" she asked, and she seemed very agitated.

"No Mum," said Soggy. "I thought she was with you."

Molly turned to Ben. "Have you seen her Ben?" Ben blushed at this. "No, Mrs Sollis, I haven't seen her at all.'

"Wherever can she be?" asked Molly. "She went out before breakfast and I haven't seen her since. Has anyone seen her?"

Harry surprised them all. "I spoke to her on the pitch this morning and she seemed right fed up to me."

"She's been like that ever since the dinner," said Soggy.

"It's not like her to go off," said Molly. "Not for a whole day, anyway."

"Don't worry, Mrs Sollis," said Mr Robson, "she'll turn up."

Molly shook her head. "It's not like her," she repeated. "I don't understand her leaving this behind. Slept in it, she did. She was frightened of losing it." Molly showed them the necklace with the little footballers on it.

"Where was it Mum?" asked Soggy.

"Well, that's the bit I really don't understand. She'd ironed all your football shirts and they were in a neat pile on the kitchen table, and this," she held the necklace up again, "was curled up on top of them."

Harry looked at it. "She had it on when I spoke to her this morning."

Mr Dyker looked worried. "Now, what did you say to her Harry?" he asked.

"Nothing much, I just told her you two had left for good and I didn't think you'd be coming back." Harry's voice got slower and slower as he went on. "I mean, that's what I thought then, you hadn't come back, you see. I just had to tell her the truth, didn't I?"

"So she doesn't know we've come back?" said Mr Dyker.

Harry shook his head.

"What shall we do, Dad?" asked Ben.

"We'll have to start looking for her," said Mr Dyker. "Come on." He opened the door of the landrover, then turned to Molly. "You stay behind, Mrs Sollis, in case she comes back."

She nodded to him, biting her lip.

"Who's coming, you lads?" They all clambered into the landrover. Nicky came running up, he'd been doing his homework and one of the other lads had told him what had happened.

"I'll follow in my car," said Mr Robson. "Any of you lads want to travel with me?" The boys already in the back of the landrover shook their heads. Mr Robson raced off to start his car, flashed his lights at Mr Dyker from the car park and the convoy was ready to move off.

Mr Dyker's knuckles were white from the force of his grip on the steering wheel. He threw the landrover into the first bend, opposite the church, the tyres screeching. The boys in the back fell on each other, then fell the other way on the next bend. The road soon became bumpy, and the lads in the back were bouncing up and down on the hard seats, trying to steady themselves. Soggy was going up and down like a yoyo, his bottom adding to the metal fatigue of the seat beneath him. The boys waved to Mr Robson out of the open back of the landrover, and he flashed his lights in return. The convoy roared on.

"We'll try that transport café on the London road first," shouted Mr Dyker to Harry, who was petrified. He clung to his seat and nodded a sickly smile. Bob was enjoying the excitement.

"That's a good idea, Dad," shouted Ben.

Mr Dyker nodded and pressed on. They had entered the dual carriageway now, and Mr Dyker built his speed up. Harry thought he would make an attempt to preserve his life. "The police patrol this stretch quite a lot, you know," he shouted. "They have radar here."

Mr Dyker shouted back. "Well, keep an eye open behind for me, will you Harry?"

Harry turned in his seat and looked back down the road. The boys in the rear saw his face set and frozen as his tried to smile at them, but it was no good. Harry muttered to himself, "They'll never catch us anyway, even if they do spot us." The convoy thundered on.

"There it is," shouted Ben. "Teas and snacks, one hundred yards."

"Good," yelled Soggy, "I'm starving." Mark clouted Soggy on the head as the convoy raced past the sign at the side of the road.

Mr Dyker started to slow down and Harry waved his arm up and down outside the passenger window. "What are you doing?" shouted Mr Dyker.

"Telling Mr Robson we're slowing down."

"I've got my indicator going and my brake lights on."

"I didn't know that, did I?"

The landrover swept into the parking area of the transport café, and threaded its way through the rows of lorries parked there, stopping outside the entrance. A crunching of gravel announced Mr Robson's arrival behind and everybody got out and marched into the building.

The place smelt of frying bacon and Soggy's nose twitched. Burly lorry drivers were eating or reading newspapers at the rows of tables leading up to the food counter. There was a juke box blaring away in the corner and a heavy fug, part cigarettes, part cooking smells, hung in the air below the yellow ceiling. Condensation ran down the walls and streaked the windows. A red-faced, sweaty, balding man leaned over his counter as they approached. He looked just like the owner of a transport café. "Are you a coach party?" he asked.

"No," replied Mr Dyker.

"We do special rates, you see."

"We're not here for food."

He pulled a face at this. "I see," he said. "Just visiting, are we?"

"We're looking for someone," shouted Soggy.

"We're looking for a girl about this high," said Mr Dyker, holding his right hand at Jacky's height. "Brown hair," he went on, "jeans and, what colour sweater did your Mum say, Soggy?"

Soggy blinked, "Yellow," he said.

The owner put his hands on the counter. "Denim jacket?" he asked, cocking his head on one side.

"Yes!" the boys chanted.

"Never heard of her," he said laughing, and then paused and looked at them all. "She was in here, this morning. Made one coffee last for hours. She had some money though."

"She's been saving up," said Soggy to Mr Dyker.

"Did she say where she was going?"

"Why don't you all sit down and have some nice cheese sandwiches and a pot of tea," the owner replied.

Mr Robson moved closer to the counter. "We haven't got time to eat anything. Can you tell us where she was headed?" Mr Robson placed two pound notes on the counter as he said this. The man placed his right hand over them before saying: "Now there's no need to do that." He turned and shouted into the back of the kitchen. "Eh, John, where did that kid say she wanted a lift to, this morning?"

John poked his head round the doorway, a chef's hat, covered in

31

dirt and grease, on his head. He wiped his hands on a filthy rag, his moon face creased in concentration. "Er, London, I think. Football ground she was after. She wanted the King's Road. Right little madam she was."

"Chelsea?" asked Ben.

"Aye, that was it," said John. "She didn't know where it was. I didn't know either, never been there. I told her where Arsenal was – rubbish they are. Never go now."

Ben started to move to the doorway. "Come on, Dad," he said. "I know why she's gone there. Come on, we're wasting time here."

They all followed Ben out, except Mr Robson, who turned to the owner and said: "Thanks a lot, you've really helped us."

"Not at all, it's a pleasure," he said, nodding at the two pound notes. "There's no need to do that, you know."

Mr Robson called his bluff. "Are you sure?" he said, with a huge smile. "That's very kind of you," and he picked up the money and left the man standing behind his counter looking very put out.

Outside Ben was explaining to his father: "I told her about Jack Hardy, Dad."

"Why did you do that, son?"

Ben was fishing for words. "I told her he was your mate, and the only . . . er physiotherapist who could help you with your leg."

Mr Dyker was puzzled. "Why did you tell her all that?" he asked.

Ben shrugged it off. "Well," he began, "we just got talking, you know."

Mr Dyker looked at Ben. "What else did you tell her?"

"Well, it's the only er . . ." Ben stumbled. "He's the only mate you've got. He was your best man, and the only pro you've kept in touch with."

"Yes, but why should she try to get there?"

Ben was in deep now. "Er, well," he began. "I, er . . . told her, whenever we hit a really bad time, trouble, you know, we always seem to end up talking to Jack Hardy at Chelsea, and he has a go at your leg and . . ."

Mr Dyker stopped Ben by putting his hand on his shoulder, "And you sit in the corner sucking Jack's Everton toffees, listening to us," he said.

Ben grinned, "Yeah."

"Right," said Mr Dyker, "that's the mystery solved. She's trying to find us and we now know where she's headed for. Follow us, Mr Robson."

Mr Dyker and Ben got into the landrover, Harry and all the other boys, some rubbing their backsides, tried to fit into Mr Robson's car. The suspension sagged and Mr Robson couldn't get into the front seat to drive. Ben and his father looked at the empty rear of their landrover and then at each other. They could see Mr Robson struggling to get in his own car. It was no good, and he yanked Dolly, Nicky, Soggy and Niggle out and banished them to the landrover. Ben and Mr Dyker stared straight ahead, trying to keep their faces composed, as the boys settled into the back. Mr Dyker started the engine and turned round to the boys. "Comfy?" he asked. This made Ben guffaw. Mr Dyker tore through the car park and out on to the main road.

Inside Mr Robson's car, Harry was bringing Mr Robson up to date on driving procedures. "You don't want to get too near him," he said. "He's a maniac."

"He's a good driver."

"Not in my book," said Harry. "You would be well advised to steer well clear of him."

Mr Robson turned to Harry. "Do you drive, Harry?" he asked.

"Never in my life."

"Ah," said Mr Robson, "that explains it."

"Look at him now," said Harry.

Mr Dyker had changed lanes to overtake a gaggle of small cars. "He's allowed to do that," replied Mr Robson.

"He's all over the road," continued Harry. "Why do you think all the kids got in here?"

Mr Robson smiled. "It's a hard ride."

"You can say that again," said Harry and started to sulk.

Mr Dyker led Mr Robson down the motorway, and on through the outskirts of London, to Baker Street. They travelled down it together, catching every green traffic light. Mr Dyker threaded the convoy round Marble Arch and down Park Lane, into the park and out at the first traffic lights. By this time Harry was going dizzy. They whizzed down to Sloane Square, round it and into the King's Road. "I know where I am now," said Harry.

"Where?" asked Mr Robson.

"The Elephant and Castle," said Harry. "Know it anywhere."

Within minutes they were at the gates to Stamford Bridge. Mr Dyker drove the landrover in and Mr Robson followed. The boys clambered out and looked about them. A large gateman came over, his bull neck falling over the collar of his dark blue security uniform. "And what do you think you're doing?" he thundered. "You can't park here. Players and officials only."

The boys backed away from him. Mr Dyker stood his ground. "Is Jack Hardy giving treatment today?"

"And what if he is?" asked the gateman.

"I'd like to see him."

"Know him, do you?"

"Yes, I do," said Mr Dyker.

The gateman looked at him, sizing him up. "We get a lot of loonies here you see. Do you know where to go?"

Mr Dyker nodded.

"Ask the kids to behave themselves."

Mr Dyker looked at the "kids". "Did you hear the gentleman?"

"Yes," they all chanted.

"I'll stay here," said Mr Robson.

Mr Dyker nodded and moved off towards the buildings at the far end of the ground. Harry and the others followed.

Four

Mr Dyker led the group across the courtyard and down behind the stand, walking underneath the huge cantilevered concrete arches. They could see the neat rows of the seats, tier upon tier. Soggy was walking along, mouth open, staring upwards. He went the wrong way, of course, and Nicky rescued him. The boys spoke in whispers and the huge deserted stand seemed to still hold the presence of thousands of spectators. Mark looked at Nicky, "It's eerie, isn't it Nick?"

"No Chelsea," said Nicky, with a straight face, and the others laughed.

Mr Dyker had stopped outside a door marked "private" and turned to the lads. "No messing about mind, no skylarking, right?"

"Right, Mr Dyker," they shouted back.

Mr Dyker pushed the door open, stepped inside and the boys followed him down a whitewashed corridor. He stopped again outside a door which had "Home Team" written on it, knocked and went in. The boys stood gawping in the entrance. The room was enormous for a dressing room, they could see showers and bathrooms leading off it. Round the walls were wooden benches, and the room was full of the first team players, milling about in a hurry to get away after the training session. Jack Hardy was working at the treatment table on a player's right ankle. He twisted it this way and that, the player pleading with him to stop. The other players laughed. "You give it to him, Jack," they shouted. "Make him suffer."

Jack turned and saw the group at the door. He slapped the player's ankle. "It's coming on a treat," he said. "You can put all your weight on it now. I'll tell the boss you're back in business, OK?" The player fled. Jack straightened up, cleaning the grease off his hands with a small towel. He nodded at Mr Dyker and smiled. "Hello stranger!"

Mr Dyker smiled back. "I hope it's not a bad time, Jack?"

"When is it a good time?" asked Jack Hardy.

Some of the team were buffeting the boys, standing in the doorway,

35

to get out. "Bye Jack." "See you." "Goodbye old icy fingers," they called, throwing their coats on and pushing and shoving like kids. As the players were leaving. Jack shouted after them: "No fags, you lot, remember, no fags."

The players groaned, "Aye, right Jack, just cigars, right!"

Jack threw his towel at them and it hit Soggy, he was thrilled. He caught it with his mouth. "And no heavy booze, you lot," called Jack. The players groaned even louder, and with laughs and jokes and pushing and messing about, they disappeared down the corridor. The echoes from their departure boomed round the boys' ears. Some of the men were playing leap frog. Soggy turned to Nicky, "They're worse than us, aren't they Nick? That feller said no skylarking."

Mr Dyker and Jack were shaking hands. "You're working late, Jack," said Mr Dyker.

"Come on," said Jack, nodding to the table, "on you get."

Mr Dyker slipped his pants down and got a cheer from the lads for his red underpants. Harry was disgusted, but only at the colour, he never wavered in his support of Everton.

Jack was making Mr Dyker's face crease up in pain as he probed and twisted with his stubby fingers. The damaged leg looked thin and wasted against the good one. Jack's red hair flopped about his good-natured lined face, the sweat beaded up on his brow and his eyes were intense as he felt for the damaged tissue underneath the bone of Mr Dyker's right leg. He looked across at Ben. "Hello youngster," he called.

"Hello, Mr Hardy," said Ben and grinned at him.

"That's what's missing here," said Jack. "Courtesy, and respect. 'Old cold hands.' 'Old freeze fingers' they call me. Disgusting!" he smiled, and looked down at Mr Dyker's screwed up face. "How've you been?" he asked.

"Fair, fair," grunted Mr Dyker, with difficulty, "I'm not complaining, anyway."

Jack bent the leg, "You've been working this haven't you?"

Mr Dyker nodded. "I've been running with the lads."

"It's better than last time, why don't you try the op?"

"You know why," replied Mr Dyker.

"Why?" whispered Soggy to Ben.

"It might go wrong," said Ben.

"Oh," said Soggy.

Jack looked at the boys, "Some toffees, you lads?" he shouted.

"Yes please, Mr Hardy," the lads chorused back.

He smiled and looked at Ben. "You know where they are Ben."

Ben went to a large cupboard in the corner and took out a huge square tin of toffees and started to hand them round. "Who are you all then?" asked Jack.

There was a chorus of "Brenton Boys' first team."

Jack smiled at the noise, and looked at Harry, his teeth wrestling with a toffee and his face showing the awe of being in a professional club's dressing room, his cap in his hand. "What position do you play?" asked Jack, with a grin. The toffee stopped Harry from answering. He just smiled and shifted from one foot to the other, and dropped his raincoat.

"He's my chief scout," said Mr Dyker.

Jack nodded, "Sit down, make yourself at home." Harry sat on the edge of one of the benches, bolt upright, recording every detail of his visit. Jack turned to Mr Dyker. "What's gone wrong now, then?"

"Nothing really, everything's fine."

"That's a change," said Jack.

"Ask Mr Hardy, Dad," shouted Ben.

"Hello, hello," said Jack. "Come on, out with it."

"We're looking for a young girl," said Mr Dyker, "Jacky Sollis. She's run off and we think she's making for here."

'Why's that?" said Jack.

"She thought *we* were coming here," replied Mr Dyker.

"Well you have."

"Yes, I know, but we are looking for her now," agreed Mr Dyker.

"I see," said Jack, giving up completely.

"It's a long story," said Mr Dyker. "She knows we show up here now and again, and we hoped she'd have got here by now."

Jack shook his head. "All I've seen today are moaning players going on about their aches and pains and why does Alan Ball always get his picture on the sports page."

Mr Dyker raised himself on his elbows. "You haven't seen her?"

"No, sorry," replied Jack. "Done a bunk, has she?"

Soggy shouted. "She's my sister."

Jack turned and looked at him. "I don't blame her for running away then." The boys all laughed.

"Eh, mister," shouted Soggy. "Will you have a look at my neck?"

The other lads jumped on him. "Shut up Soggy, he doesn't want to die of shock!" "He won't be able to see it for dirt!"

"What's the matter with it?" asked Jack.

Soggy rolled his head gently. "Well, it goes all stiff like, you know."

"Is it worse in the morning?" asked Jack.

"Yes," said Soggy, wonder on his face. "How did you know?"

Jack smiled. "Come here." Jack sat Soggy on a chair. He pushed his head forward, and placed Soggy's elbows on his knees. Then he said gently, "What programmes did you watch last night?"

Soggy went through his list. "Er, the cartoon, Jackanory, boring that was. The News, Nationwide, then there was a play on but none of us could understand it, lots of boobies and men shouting." The boys roared with laughter. "Then the news came on again," continued Soggy. "Then something about fishing, then we had our cocoa."

Jack felt the back of Soggy's neck. "Did you move about at all?" he enquired.

"No," said Soggy, "I keep very still, sometimes people think I'm dead."

Jack shook his head with disbelief. "Can I give you a little advice son?"

"See a doctor?" asked Soggy.

"No," said Jack. "At the end of each programme just roll your neck round, like this." Jack did a neck roll for Soggy.

"Thanks mister."

"Not at all," replied Jack.

"Shall I do it now," asked Soggy.

"Why not," said Jack, and gave up.

Just at that moment the large gateman came into the dressing room, breathing heavily. "Hello Bill," said Jack. "Did you want something?"

Bill glared about him and said. "A kid has sneaked through the main gate and run across the pitch. I thought he might be with you lot."

Ben pricked his ears up. "Did he have a yellow sweater and a denim jacket?" he asked.

"Yes," replied Bill, "long hair down to his shoulders. Is he with you?"

All the lads started to smile and nod at each other. "Yes," said Ben, grinning, "*he's* with us."

38

"Well, could you find him quickly," said Bill, his face worried now.

"Why," asked Jack, "what's the matter?"

"Sheba's loose in the ground. Tom's off for his break and she won't return for me." Bill dropped his eyes. "She's slipped her lead."

Mr Dyker sat up on the table. "What's all this about, Jack?"

"The guard dog," said Jack, biting his lip. "We've had a bit of nonsense, people breaking in you know. She's allowed to roam when the gates are shut, when everybody's gone."

The boys looked at each other, Bomber shivered, he hated dogs. The room went very quiet. "Does it attack?" asked Mr Dyker softly.

Jack nodded, "It's very good at it."

"Oh no!" exclaimed Mr Dyker, scrambling off the table. "Come on, let's find her."

"Her?" asked Bill.

"Yes," shouted Nicky. "She's a girl."

Mr Dyker was scrambling into his clothes now. "That dog is vicious," said Bill. "She's all right on the lead, but off it, she's uncontrollable except by Tom."

"Where's Tom gone?" asked Jack.

"Home."

"Is he on the phone?"

"No," said Bill, gloomily.

Mr Dyker forced his way out of the dressing room. "Come on," he shouted, "let's find where she is. If she keeps still we've got a chance."

All the boys, Harry, Jack and the gateman followed Mr Dyker out of the room and down the corridor. Once in the ground, they looked towards the cars where Mr Robson stood, waving to them. "Any joy yet?" he shouted.

Mr Dyker cupped his hands in front of his mouth to make his voice carry. "Yes," he called. "She's here, but there's a guard dog loose, and the handler is out of the ground. We've got to try and find her."

Mr Robson gulped and looked about him, then waved to let them know he'd understood. Very carefully he started to walk towards them, as the group moved down to the barriers at the foot of the stand. They all looked at the vast arena, trying to spot a bit of movement, a flash of yellow, anything. The ground was deserted except for themselves, the stands silent and empty. A seagull detached itself lazily from the roof of the stand at the far end of the pitch, and flew slowly down towards them, then flicked a wing and was up and away over the offices. They watched it go. "Where do we start?" asked Mr Robson.

"God knows," answered Mr Dyker, shaking his head.

Ben leapt over the barrier and ran on to the pitch. He started to shout, "Jacky! Jacky!" Moving into the centre, twisting and turning as he ran, to see into the four corners of the ground.

"Right!" said Mr Dyker, and clambered over the barrier, the others following him. They ran and joined Ben. Their voices, faint now, drifted on the wind, up and away like the seagull. They peered about shading their eyes to look at the top rows of seats, but it was hopeless. "Jacky! Jacky!" they shouted, but nobody answered.

Soggy was looking tense, the colour had drained from his face and he was near to tears. Mr Robson put his hand on his shoulder and shouted with him: "Jacky! Jacky!"

 The low growl made Jacky catch her breath, as she watched the alsatian's jaws drip with saliva. Another wild, low growl made her hair stand on end, and she shuddered. The dog saw the movement and edged forward, eyes fixed on Jacky. She was trapped in a corner, half-way up the big centre stand, and she was terrified. The dog had chased her along the rows of seats, snapping at her heels, and she was exhausted. Suddenly, Jacky saw something move on the pitch, and she could faintly hear someone chanting her name. She forced herself to focus, through her tears, on the movement on the pitch, and made out Mr Dyker and the group of boys. Her heart turned over. The dog's growl had changed, and was getting higher pitched and longer. It was working itself up to spring.

Jacky's courage deserted her, she threw her head back and screamed at the top of her voice. Eyes shut, she screamed and screamed. The sudden noise made the dog back away onto its haunches. It also drew the attention of the group on the pitch. Ben's eyes whipped round to the centre stand, and he could see Jacky's arms waving above the crash barrier.

"There she is, Dad," he shouted. "Look, she's over there, in the middle."

They all looked in the direction Ben was pointing. Jacky's thin arms and long hair could be clearly seen now.

40

The group ran to the foot of the stand, where Mr Dyker held them back, shouting up to Jacky. "Keep still, keep still. Don't move, Jacky, we're coming!"

Bill shouted up: "Hold Sheba, hold Sheba. Sheba, steady girl, steady." The dog pricked up its ears and started to growl again at Jacky.

"He's going to jump," shouted Jacky. "Help, oh please help, he's going to jump!"

"What do we do now?" asked Mr Robson.

Jack Hardy turned to Bill. "What does Tom give her when he's working her, Bill?"

"Chocolate," answered Bill. "Bits of chocolate, she goes mad for it."

Ben whispered in Soggy's ear. Soggy nodded and produced a large bar of chocolate from his windcheater. Ben whipped it out of his hand and went haring up the steps of the stand like a gazelle, his long hair billowing behind him.

"Come back, Ben, come back," shouted Mr Dyker.

Ben half raised his right hand, without slackening pace or turning round. The others stood and watched. The dog heard Ben coming and turned to look at him, then faced Jacky again. Ben stopped about twenty feet away, behind the dog. Jacky raised her terrified face to Ben. The dog didn't know what to do, she turned her head backwards and forwards at both of them. Then she decided on Ben, and slowly padded towards him. Ben froze. "Climb over the gangway Jacky. Make towards my dad," he said. "Softly, slowly, Jacky. Go on, slowly."

"Oh, Ben," whimpered Jacky, and started to stand up. The dog did nothing, intent now on Ben. Jacky climbed swiftly over the low concrete wall, and with her fear helping her to break the sound barrier, she hopped and skipped down the stepped terrace to the watching group below. The dog turned and saw her go, then faced Ben. I've had it thought Ben. She's going for me any minute. "Here, Sheba, here, Sheba," he croaked, unwrapping the chocolate. "Here boy . . . er girl, good girl, Sheba, good girl. Good Sheba." Ben threw a piece of chocolate at the dog. Sheba stopped her slow crawl forward and pricked her ears up, confused by the smell of chocolate. Ben threw a piece nearer. Sheba was westling with her training and her belly, her belly won. She licked the chocolate and swallowed it. Ben heard his father shout, "Don't turn your back on her, Ben, be careful."

"Good girl, Sheba. Who's a good girl then?" asked Ben, croaking away. A little more confident now, he threw another piece of Soggy's life-saving iron rations behind Sheba, who turned and padded towards it. Ben threw the lot after her and raced down to the others, two steps at a time.

Their faint cheer got louder and louder, as Ben rocketed down to them, grinning all over his face. He cannoned into them, but Jack Hardy fielded him beautifully, swinging him round to slow him up. Jacky had been swept up by Mr Dyker, her tears of fright nearly gone now. "Come on dry your eyes, little one," said Mr Dyker. "It's all right now, it's all right!"

"I came to tell you about the field," sobbed Jacky. "Mr Owen said we can have it. It would make a good pitch."

"We know, we know," replied Mr Dyker.

"We've seen it," said Ben.

"Harry said you had gone for good," accused Jacky.

Mr Dyker looked at Mr Robson. "Well we haven't, so dry your eyes and cheer up."

"All the parents are mucking in to get a pitch ready," shouted Nicky. "So we can qualify for the League, Jacky."

"You shut up, Nicky Brown," she said.

Nicky looked at the others. "What have I done?" he asked.

Mr Dyker winked at him. Bill was gazing with wonder at Ben. "I'm amazed," he said. "That dog has had the Chairman, he won't get out of his car now. You're very lucky young man, er lady, very lucky!"

Jack clapped his hands together. "How about some tea, eh? I think we could all do with something after that little lot."

"That's very kind of you, Jack," said Mr Dyker.

Soggy was on the outside of the group. "Has anyone got any more chocolate?" he asked plaintively. The group moaned.

"It went in a good cause, Soggy. You'll get some more," said Bomber.

"You're always thinking of your belly," shouted Nicky.

"It's not for me," said Soggy.

"Oh, yes," the others shouted in derision. "We've heard that one before!"

42

"It's for Sheba," shouted Soggy.

The others turned and looked at him. He had taken his belt off and slipped it through Sheba's collar. She sat looking at them, tongue hanging out, very much the household pet. The group didn't believe her, they broke up like banshies, men as well as the team, and raced headlong down the touchline to the safety of the tunnel. Soggy shouted after them: "It's all right, she's all right now. You have to be firm. She's all right now, aren't you Sheba . .? Sheba . .? Sheba . .?"

The dog growled ever so softly, and Soggy, ever so slowly, walked her after the others. She stopped every now and again and growled. So did Soggy, he had to. He spoke to her softly, promising her more chocolate, and she went quietly along as though she believed him.

Five

Jack Hardy was being everybody's favourite uncle, and gave the team a grand tour of the ground. They had even been into the Boardroom, and Soggy had sat in the Chairman's imposing chair and sacked all the players. They had enjoyed the tea Jack laid on, and old Bill, a great friend now, had slipped out for a load of cakes. He was so grateful that Sheba hadn't had someone's leg for her tea. Jack showed the boys all the trophies and medals, the lists of past players and old photographs. Mr Dyker was on one of the photographs with his arm around Jack, for they had played together very often. Mr Dyker held the photo for a long time until he felt Ben looking at him, then he smiled sheepishly and placed it back with the others.

Harry kept asking, "Who does all the polishing?"

"Looking for a job, mate?" asked Jack.

"I'd be over the moon," replied Harry. "Anything to get away from the Mrs. I'm not sure about Bob, though, me dog you know."

"Why?" said Jack. "Nervous of Sheba?"

"Yes, Bob might kill the stupid thing." Everybody laughed.

All this time Jacky kept glancing at Ben a flashing big "thank you's" with her eyes. Ben kept blushing.

Jack led them all over the ground, until finally they stood in the gloom of the tunnel that led out to the pitch. Jack held his hand up. "Well lads, this is where they run out on to the pitch, every Saturday. First team or second, there's always twelve players wearing Chelsea colours going out there." Jack nodded to the pitch and turned to Mr Dyker. "Do you miss it, Alan?"

Mr Dyker smiled, "What do you think?"

Mr Robson came bustling up. "I've rung up your mother, Jacky," he said. "She's very relieved to know you are all right." Mr Robson put his hand on Jacky's shoulder and leaned over to whisper to her. "She's very angry with you Jacky."

Jacky bit her bottom lip and nodded, then burst into tears again.

Soggy threw his head back at this and appealed to the rest of the lads. "Honestly," he said loudly, "would you believe it! Girls!"

"Shut up Soggy," said Ben.

Soggy back-pedalled right away. "Right, Ben, right," he stuttered. "Sorry, our Jacky," he said, throwing her a grubby handkerchief.

She sniffed and threw it back at him.

"She doesn't cry at home you know, Ben, so don't be taken in by her."

"Soggy!" warned Ben.

"Right, Ben, right. I'm only trying to put things right."

Jack Hardy astounded them all by saying: "Have you all got track shoes on?"

"Yes," "Always," "What else?" was the chorus back.

Jack beamed at them. "Would you like to have a kick about?" he asked.

The boys didn't believe him. "What, on the pitch?" "Do you mean it mister?" "You're joking, aren't you?"

Jack smiled at Mr Dyker. "No, I'm not joking." He pointed to a door at the far end of the tunnel. "There's a ball in there Ben, just inside the doorway. Bring it out, would you?"

Ben raced off to get the ball with the boys watching him. Mr Dyker moved over to Jack and shook his head, grinning. "One minute these kids haven't got anywhere to play and the next they're kicking about on a first division pitch."

"That's life, me old china," said Jack. "Wonderful, isn't it, eh?"

Ben threw the ball at Jack, who caught it and bounced it up and down on the concrete floor. The boys were straining to get on to the pitch and started to shuffle forward, elbows going, to get there first. Jack took command. "Eh! Eh!" he shouted. "Just a minute, just a minute! Let's have a bit of respect, shall we? Line up, come on, line up." He pushed and shoved the boys into an excited line. Ben at the front, followed by Mark, then Soggy, Nick, and the rest of them. Mr Hardy walked up and down like a sergeant major. He threw his shoulders back and strutted in front of them. "There's eighty thousand people out there, come to see you play," he thundered. "Let's get those heads up. Come on, let's have some style." The boys grinned at him and smartened themselves up.

Jack seemed satisfied. He led them out and shouted over his shoulder. "Bow to Her Majesty. No scratching, no picking your noses, no spitting. Don't look at the cameras and no selfish play. Do you hear me Chelsea?"

"No! Brenton! Brenton!" shouted the boys.

"OK," said Jack, "Brenton. Come on!" He broke into a run and the boys followed. They raced to the far goal, tapping the ball to each other. Nicky touched the goal post first. Harry had been enjoying Jack's bit of fun with the team. He glanced over to Mr Dyker to see his reaction.

Mr Dyker was walking slowly after the boys, with Harry just a little to one side of him, his mind miles away. In his head he could hear the fans shouting and roaring away as the boys cleared the tunnel and burst into the sunlight. Harry saw him lift his head and gaze at the empty terraces. To Mr Dyker they were packed, full of waving fans, shouting encouragement. Mr Dyker's eyes were bright with excitement, his body began to twitch. He started to move faster and broke into a run. His right leg slowed him to a halt, immediately. He hopped on to it as he stopped and grinned sheepishly at Harry.

Harry pretended not to notice. "I never thought I'd be treading this turf at my age," Harry said, looking the other way.

Mr Dyker leaned on Harry. "It's quite a feeling, Harry, isn't it? Never leaves you, you know." Mr Dyker looked about him and sighed. "I've played here once or twice."

Harry stopped and looked at him. "Well, I'll be blowed," he said. "There's hope for you yet!"

"What do you mean?"

Harry started to walk on again. "That's the first time I've heard you talk about your playing days."

"Well," said Mr Dyker, "you can't live in the past all the time, can you?"

"I have to."

Mr Dyker shook his head. "You're an old fox Harry, do you know that?"

"Aye," said Harry.

The ball came bouncing towards them. Jack Hardy had seen them ambling along and robbed Soggy of the ball, belting it down the pitch towards them. Mr Dyker hopped about to control the ball.

He stopped it well and wriggled to get it on his good foot. "Come on Dyker!" shouted Jack. "Get a move on."

Mr Dyker grinned and hit the ball with his left foot, straight to Ben, who found the goal first time with it. Jack shouted to him. "You're nearly as good as your dad."

"Ah, eh!" shouted Harry. "Let's score a goal, go on. I've always wanted to do that. I'll take a penalty, eh?"

"Right!" shouted Jack. "In goal Boggy."

"Soggy!" laughed the lads. Soggy rolled his trousers up to his knees and ran between the goal posts. He started to tremble in mock fear, as Harry placed the ball on the spot and walked back to take the kick. Harry addressed them all. "The ambition of a lifetime this, you know. We never had it like this when we were kids." Harry looked at the empty stands and shouted. "Pay attention you lot, you won't see the likes of this too often." He waved his arms at the imaginary crowd, polished his right shoe on his trouser leg and looked at Soggy. "Are you ready, Gordon Banks?"

"Who's that?" said Soggy.

"A famous jockey," shouted Nicky, and fell over laughing.

Harry ran up to the ball and clouted it very hard. Soggy had no chance, the ball sped past him for a good goal. Harry's shoe didn't though. He was even more accurate with that, it hit Soggy right on the head. The team applauded. Harry hopped about with his arms high in the air. "What a goal! What a goal!" he shouted.

Soggy climbed up to the cross bar and put Harry's shoe there. "That'll learn you. That'll learn you," he shouted.

Jack Hardy was laughing his head off, as he reached up and retrieved Harry's shoe for him, and offered to sign him on. Harry agreed terms right away, then bent to put his shoe on again.

They kicked in for a little while longer, with Jack and Mr Dyker in goal, behaving like two big kids, roaring away, shouting at near misses, pushing each other over. Ben stood and watched his father enjoying himself. He felt good. If only it could be like this all the time, he thought, then he shook himself, as the ball arrived at his feet. Ben hit a long curling shot into the top corner, and Jack punched it away. Mr Dyker jumped on Jack and wrestled him to the ground. All the team raced up and threw themselves on top, even Jacky. Harry looked at Mr Robson, they smiled at each other as the mass of bodies in front of them heaved and tossed about. Harry nodded at the mound, "Looks like a bit of aggro in the goal mouth," he said. "Animals! I don't know what the game is coming to!"

Back home in Brenton, strange and wonderful things were happening on Donald Owen's field. Huge earth-moving machines were already at the bottom end of the pitch to begin the levelling. A prehistoric looking "ditcher" was starting a drainage system from the top end. Two tractors fussed about with the huge tree trunk in the middle of the pitch. Mr Baker was astride a large farm mowing machine. He looked back at the straight swathe he had cut through the outside of the proposed pitch. Not bad for a welder he thought. If only those fools would get rid of that tree in the middle, I could lay all the grass. He saw someone come running up to him out of the corner of his eye, and throttled the lurching machinery down to a tolerable level. It was Molly, her eyes wide with amazement. "What are you all doing?" she shouted above the din.

He smiled down at her. "Well, we all got together when the lads went off, and decided to make a start tonight. Well, I made them really," he said. "There's nothing on the telly and you and I both know, Molly, unless we start right away, we'll still be talking about it in a week's time." He looked about him from his lofty perch, and went on. "So I've got them at it."

Molly turned and looked at the feverish activity going on round the field. "Quite keen, aren't they," he said.

Molly was thrilled to bits. "Oh, the boys will be pleased."

Mr Baker lit his pipe, and the blue smoke drifted over the bonnet of the mower, and swirled down to mingle with the sweet smell of the cut grass. "Any news about Jacky?" he asked carefully.

"That's what I've come to tell you," said Molly excitedly, "they've found her! I've had a call from Mr Robson and they're on their way back. She'd gone all the way to London."

"To see the Queen?" asked Mr Baker, laughing at the good news.

"No," said Molly. "To see Chelsea Football ground."

"Whatever made her go there?"

"No idea," said Molly.

"They can't play for toffee," he went on. "Spurs I could understand, but not that lot."

Molly frowned. "Anyway she's safe, and so are the boys."

48

He nodded and placed his thumb over the glowing tobacco, pressing it tight down the bowl. Molly winced.

"Good," he said. "We'll have something to show them when they get back." He looked over to the tree trunk party. "Come on Brian," he shouted to Mr Woodgate. "That's the sixth fag you've had, put your back into it." Brian waved back at him, they could hear his chuckle carried faintly to them through the cranking and coughing of the tractors. "I'm enjoying this," said Mr Baker. "It's like playing with mud pies again." His eyes twinkled down to Molly, "I'll shake this lot up. Come on, you volunteers," he shouted. "We've got another hour's good light yet, then you can go and have your pints." A big cheer went up. "All on Brian," he shouted. A big groan went up this time.

"I hope the boys appreciate what you're doing for them," said Molly.

"Listen Molly, the way those lads played in that final, winning the League and the Cup, then having their pitch whipped away from them, I'm glad to do it. They've earned it, they've dragged themselves off the floor, those lads." He puffed away at his pipe.

"It's a higher league they're trying for now, isn't it?" said Molly.

"Aye, the County League, it's a hard one," he said, "big lads. We've never been good enough to get in it before."

"They'll have to win it for you, after all you are doing for them."

"We won't settle for less, Molly. The winners go to Germany in a friendly – have a fortnight there, did you know that?"

Molly shook her head.

"Oh, aye," he went on. "They tour all over. Nothing like it when I was a lad." He knocked his pipe out and smiled at her. "Well, I must get on. Mind out, Molly, this thing throws up a lot of muck." He pushed the throttle and the huge mower thundered forward. Molly moved backwards and waved at him. He only nodded, he wasn't clever enough to take his hands off the controls just yet. He let in the clutch, and the machine took him for a grass-eating walk. His pipe bounced out of his pocket and was shredded quite nicely. Brian saw this, and shook with laughter.

Outside the ground the boys stood in a respectful group. Mr Dyker shook hands with Jack Hardy, and thanked him for his kindness. Jack shook hands with all of them, slowly and solemnly. "You've got a good right foot there, youngster," he said to Harry. Harry just nodded his thanks to him. Soggy swore later that Harry had a tear in his eye. But as Harry's eyes watered a bit in winter, he wasn't too sure. The boys gave Jack a cheer. "Good luck with your pitch," he shouted. "Let me know when it's ready and I'll come along and roast you." The boys laughed and climbed into the landrover and Mr Robson's car. "Goodbye Jack." "Goodbye Mr Hardy," shouted everybody, and they drove off. Jack watched them hurtle down the Fulham Road, then went to his own car.

Jacky didn't seem keen to get home too quickly, fearing her mother's anger. But the journey back was faster and Harry aged at least forty years. Mr Robson insisted on keeping up with the Dyker's Monte Carlo Grand Prix entry, and this proved rather exciting at times.

The convoy slammed round Brenton, dropping the boys off at intervals. "See you tomorrow at training," they shouted to each other, and raced indoors. Jacky and Soggy were last. Mr Robson had taken Harry and his car-load of lads home.

Molly was standing on her front step as the landrover drew up. Jacky flew down the path and Molly held her very tightly. "It's all right. It's all right," she kept saying, smoothing Jacky's hair and drying her eyes on her cooking apron. Molly heard the landrover start to rev up and waved, gesturing for Mr Dyker and Ben to come in. They looked at each other, then Mr Dyker switched the engine off and followed Soggy indoors.

It was a clean and tidy house, everything sparkled and there was a pleasant smell of furniture polish, mingling with the smell of supper. They waited in the hall until Molly came downstairs and invited them both to stay and share the food. Ben was famished and couldn't wait to sit down. Soggy was led off to the scullery to wash his hands. "Come on Jacky," shouted Molly, "we've got guests. Stop hiding yourself away up there." At long last they heard Jacky come down the stairs and she followed Soggy into the scullery to help her mother.

Mr Dyker and Ben looked at each other across the dining-table.

Mr Dyker touched the spotless tablecloth and smiled at Ben. "I told you we'd have a proper tablecloth, didn't I?" he whispered. Ben smiled.

"I don't care what you say, Crispin, just you wash those hands again," shouted Molly. Ben started to giggle.

"They had genuine Chelsea mud on them, they did," complained Soggy, over the noise of the running tap.

"I don't care what they had on them, you're not sitting down with dirty hands. What will Mr Dyker think?"

Ben and his father quickly checked the colour of their own hands and Mr Dyker raised his eyebrows at Ben to make him show his. They looked fairly clean so Mr Dyker let him off. Molly came bustling in with extra knives and forks and caught them both showing each other their hands. She smiled and pretended not to notice. Jacky brought in two heaped plates of shepherd's pie. She placed one in front of Ben. "Jacky!" scolded Molly, "you should have served Mr Dyker first."

"Sorry Mam," said Jacky, and gave Mr Dyker his and ran back into the scullery.

"She's always doing that," said Soggy, "isn't she, Ben?"

Ben squirmed about a bit then said. "No, er, I wouldn't say that."

"Well, I would," said Soggy. "Where's mine then?"

Jacky had returned with her mother's and her own supper and was now sitting down looking at Ben. "You can get your own."

Soggy moaned and groaned and went to get his supper. Mr Dyker smiled at Molly, and they all began a very late supper.

"I'm glad you could stay for supper, Mr Dyker," she said.

"Not at all," mumbled Mr Dyker, caught between mouthfuls of gravy and potato. "We're very glad to accept, aren't we Ben?"

"Yes," said Ben brightly, "it's a change from my cooking. This is very good Mrs Sollis."

Molly beamed. "Well, what a long day it's been." Then her hand flew to her mouth at her forgetfulness. "Oh, would you like a beer, Mr Dyker?"

"That would be very nice, yes please," answered Mr Dyker, frowning at Ben, who was digging a potato island for his gravy, between large mouthfuls.

"Can I have one?" pleaded Soggy.

"No, you can't," said Molly firmly.

"I'm allowed cider though, aren't I Mum? I mean, when we've got some. It's great having people in to dinner, isn't it Mum?"

Jacky threw a "please put up with the local loony" look to Ben and said: "Soggy, do try to behave sensibly."

"Behave?" echoed Soggy. "Behave! It wasn't me who ran away you know."

Molly had brought a beer, and orange juice for the children. She placed them on the table and looked at Mr Dyker. "I want to thank you, Mr Dyker," she said, "for keeping this little family together today, bringing Jacky back safely for us." Everybody looked towards the television set, but it couldn't help them, it was switched off.

"Yes, well," said Mr Dyker, moving about in his chair. "I think it's been a difficult day for all of us, eh Ben? I'm glad everything sorted itself out."

"But it was good of you, Mr Dyker," said Molly.

"It was nothing, and er, please call me Alan, Mrs Sollis."

Jacky looked across at Ben. He looked back at Jacky. Molly sat down and looked at Alan and smiled. He smiled, Ben smiled, Jacky smiled, Soggy looked amazed, as they all started grinning. "That dog was enormous, wasn't it Ben?" he said loudly.

"Oh, I wouldn't say that Crispin," replied Ben, with a straight face. But he couldn't keep it up, he laughed and so did the others, even Molly. Soggy's shepherd's pie got colder and colder as they all rocked away with laughter and relief.

Six

A few weeks later, Ben was fussing inside the caravan, waiting for his father to return for a meeting. He busied himself by arranging the drop-down table, whistling softly to himself as he placed mugs ready for the coffee his father always called for.

Outside, a bossy Harry was taking his "stand in training session for the boss", very, very seriously. Ben smiled as he heard Harry berating Soggy. "Come on, come on, get those legs up," shouted Harry. "You've got to jog one, then race one, and you're just strolling round Soggy, like a bloody Sunday walk." Harry had placed four corner flags in a twelve yard square and he had the boys running and walking round them, all except Soggy.

"You want to try this Harry," panted Mark, the sweat flying off him.

"I'm not allowed," said Harry smugly.

"How much longer?" shouted Nicky.

Harry looked at the stop watch dangling round his neck on a bootlace. "I'll tell you when, I'll tell you when," he shouted.

Soggy caught his attention again and Harry blasted him.

"Soggy!" he thundered, "you've slowed down again."

"You're supposed to take one slow," gasped Soggy.

"You're taking them all slow," screamed Harry. "You're bone idle. Let's see you run, come on."

The other boys took up the chant as they padded round the square. "Come on you idle Sogg, let's see you run, you idle Sogg! Come on you idle Sogg, let's see you run!" They got faster and faster and Soggy was forced to go with them, slipping and slithering round each corner flag.

Harry called a halt. "All right, all right, slow down," he shouted. "Slow down, come on, come on, I want you to get into a circle now."

"Get in a what?" said Nicky, playing up.

Harry looked at him sternly. "A circle lad, a circle. You know

53

what a circle is, don't you?"

"Oh, a *circle*!" breathed Nicky, with much open-mouthed wonder and head nodding.

Harry ignored him. "Get a ball, Dolly," he said. The lads stood in Harry's circle, waiting for Dolly to throw Harry the ball. "Now then," said Harry pompously, "you all know this exercise. I throw the ball at you in turn, and you chest it down or take it on your thigh or trap it, OK?"

"Can we have a rest, Harry?" asked Soggy, swaying on his feet.

"No you bloody can't. You've done nothing yet, but you keep complaining. Any more of it and I'll have you running the pitch, right?"

"Yes, Harry," said Soggy, rolling his eyes.

"Right, now then," said Harry, shuffling about to retrieve his dignity, "are you ready?" There was a general murmur of agreement and a lot of getting their breath back. Harry suddenly shouted, "Niggle!" and threw the ball at him. Niggle chested it down and kicked it back to Harry. "Dolly!" shouted Harry, and Dolly caught the ball on his thigh and returned it. Harry decided to risk it. "Soggy!" he shouted, and hurled the ball at Soggy's heaving chest. It just bounced off and rolled back to Harry. Harry threw his eyes to the sky and opened his arms to the whole of the Southern counties. "And what was that supposed to be?" The team giggled.

"I wasn't ready," said Soggy.

"Oh, I see," said Harry, "you weren't ready! Well, next time I'll send you a written invitation. Is there any danger of you being ready now?"

"Yes," said Soggy, going red.

"Right," said Harry, holding the ball on the upturned palm of his hand. "Now watch this everybody, I want you all to witness the skill of this young man." He delicately lobbed the ball on to Soggy's chest and Soggy chested it down like a professional, then booted it back to Harry. The other boys applauded his efforts. "*Very* good, *very* good," mocked Harry. "What fantastic skill! If only we could keep this player awake, we could be on to something." Just then Harry spotted the landrover turning into the field. "Right you lads," he shouted, "quick as you like, touch that bottom fence down there and back again. Come on, let's see who's the fastest."

54

Bomber shouted, "Nicky is, he always wins."

Harry blew his whistle and the boys hared off, waving at the landrover as they charged past it. Mr Dyker tooted his horn as the boys swept down the slope to the far fence. Nicky was leading, of course, his long legs going like blazes, his arms pumping away, his black hair blown back off his face for once. Now the guv'nor was watching, the boys were out to impress; it was a fair old race.

Mr Dyker stopped the landrover and he and Jacky got out. "How are they getting on, Harry?" he asked.

"Not too bad, not too bad," replied Harry, puffing his chest out.

Mr Dyker smiled at him. "You're working them well, they look keen to me."

"Aye," said Harry proudly.

"Come on then," said Mr Dyker, "let's get at it," and he led the way into the caravan, with Jacky and Harry following.

Ben had already put the steaming cups of coffee on the table and Mr Dyker picked his up, blowing across it to cool it down, leaning against the caravan wall.

"Well," he said, "she's got the letter, our little secretary."

Jacky nervously held up a long white envelope, the others sipped their coffee and stared at it. Mr Dyker took it from her and read: "County League Boy's Football Association. Very impressive." Then Mr Dyker placed the envelope carefully on the table. "This will tell us whether we are wiped out before we start."

Ben felt he could bear the suspense no longer. "Open it Dad, open it."

Mr Dyker smiled and shook his head. "Let's wait for the lads to come back. We're all in this together now." They sipped their coffee and gazed at the bright white letter with the black official printing, hoping for the best.

Harry shouted from the doorway. "They're nearly here, Nicky's in front."

"He always is," said Ben.

"Soggy's doing well," said Harry, "I'm amazed."

"There's a lot in that lad," said Mr Dyker.

"Aye," said Harry. "You should see the potatoes he gets through."

The boys were approaching now, and Mr Dyker led the group outside to see them arrive. The team were coming up the slope like heroes. Nicky in front, holding Mark off, and the rest were in a tight bunch, all of them going well, heads up, fists up to their shoulders, not a slacker among them.

Mr Dyker watched with pride as they threw themselves on the grass at the foot of the caravan steps, panting and sobbing. Bomber was making great wheezing noises. "All right, you lads," said Mr Dyker, "breathe deeply. Slow down, come on, slow . . . slow . . . deep breaths." Bomber was going puce.

"Bomber!" shouted Mr Dyker. "Have you been smoking again?"

Bomber managed to shake his head. "No, Mr Dyker," he choked. "Not since you told me."

Mr Dyker didn't believe him. "I'll drop you Bomber, I mean it." Bomber gave up smoking there and then.

"I wasn't last," shouted Soggy. "I wasn't last, Mr Dyker, Bomber was."

"I got a stitch," shouted Bomber.

"Well done lads, well done," said Mr Dyker, "you looked great! Who could do it again?" A great moan went up.

"I can, Mr Dyker," shouted Soggy, and he bounded up and was off.

"Eh! Soggy!" shouted Mr Dyker. "Come back here, I was only joking." Soggy crawled gratefully back to the group and flopped.

Mr Dyker stood looking at them for a little while, then reached inside the caravan and picked up the letter, waving it in the air. "This is the season's fixture list," he said quietly. "You all know our problems, the pitch is not ready. Everybody has worked very hard but the pitch is not ready, and without a pitch we don't qualify, we are out."

"That's not fair," said Dolly.

Mr Dyker smiled at him. "It never is lad," he said and looked at the rest of the them. "Who feels lucky?"

"What do you mean, Mr Dyker?" asked Mark.

Mr Dyker shrugged his shoulders, "Who wants to open it?" Nobody answered him, so Mr Dyker broke the silence. "If the first two games are away matches, we have a chance. If not, they'll disqualify us . . ." his words hung in the air. The boys bit their lips, scratched their noses, pulled nervous faces, studied their track shoes.

When Nicky spoke everybody jumped. "I'll open it, Mr Dyker," he said, and stood up.

"Yeah," shouted Soggy and Bomber together.

"Nicky's always lucky," shouted Adrian.

"He's won a premium bond," shouted Dolly.

"Twice!" interrupted Niggle.

"And he always picks the winner in the Grand National," said Soggy. "And anyway, I've got my fingers crossed."

Mr Dyker smiled, "We can't lose then, can we Sogg?" and he handed Nicky the long white envelope. The others watched him just as if he were defusing a bomb as he slipped his fingernail under the flap, gently prising it open. When he unfolded the single page letter a great sigh went up. Nicky read their playing future silently, his eyes giving nothing away.

"I'll give you the names in reverse order," he joked. But when he looked at their faces he couldn't pretend to be calm any longer. "It's all right, it's all right!" he said, and his voice was high with excitement. "I don't know who they are, but we're playing Woodfield and Hatton, on their grounds, in our first two matches!"

A great cheer went up as he handed the letter to Mr Dyker. Dolly and Niggle were whooping and fighting on the ground with relief, Mark and Nicky were grinning. Soggy threw his head back. "I told you he was lucky," he shouted. "I told you!"

Mr Dyker ruffled Ben's hair. Harry pinched Jacky's cheeks. Then Mark picked up the ball, booted it high into the air, and everybody broke and chased after it, exhaustion forgotten. Then they went into a lap of honour round the pitch, startling the crew of dads who were putting in an early shift on the ground.

Stan Baker heard the racket above the noise of the tractor and turned to watch the boys lunatic behaviour, his brown lined face creased into a huge grin.

"That's it, Brian," he shouted. "That's it, their first two games must be away. We're in with a chance now. Our work won't be a waste of time."

"What?" shouted Brian.

"Never mind," replied Mr Baker, "just keep working." Another load of hard core went into the hollow at the far end of the pitch and Brian bent his back and started to rake it over.

Mr Dyker, Ben, Harry and Jacky, shaded their eyes against the sunlight, as they watched the boys running round the pitch.

Mr Dyker was thrilled to bits. "We've six weeks now, we'll do it easy, Harry," and he read the letter again.

"Aye, boss, we'll do it," said Harry.

"Woodfield are playing their first game next week. Can you and Jacky go and have a look at them, tell us what they're like?"

"It'll be a pleasure, won't it Jacky?" said Harry. Jacky just nodded.

"You'll have to acknowledge this letter Jacky. Can you get a reply off?"

"Yes, Mr Dyker," said a very happy Jacky.

Mr Dyker was still scanning the letter. "It goes on about proper facilities being available for the visiting teams. We'll just have to play that by ear," he muttered.

"Does that mean changing rooms?" asked Jacky.

"Yes," replied Mr Dyker. "We'll just have to do the best we can."

Jacky looked worried. "But they won't be ready, will they?"

"No," said Mr Dyker. "But football is about a ball, twenty-two players and a clear space to run round on, and that's what they'll get."

"But Woodfield are a snooty lot," said Jacky. "If we haven't got showers and things, they'll do everything to get us out of the League."

Mr Dyker looked at her. "We'll meet that when it comes. We'll have a pitch, that's all that matters now. We can always plead ignorance."

"That's all very well Dad," said Ben, "but where will we change?"

Mr Dyker handed Jacky the letter. "The building won't be ready, right?" he said. "So we've asked Mrs Lodge to lend her marquee. She hates football, but says the thing wants airing before her garden 'do', so she's agreed to let us have it."

Jacky's face was a picture. "Of course, she lends it to the cricket lot for their teas and things."

Mr Dyker looked at Harry. "How are they getting on with the pitch, Harry?"

"Well," said Harry, "it looks a right mess now, as you can see, but when they finish levelling it and returfing here and there, it'll be great."

"Come on then," said Mr Dyker. "Let's get ready for Mr Robson, he'll be here soon."

They went inside the caravan and sat round the table. Mr Dyker started to make a list and Jacky pencilled in a rough draft of her letter to the League. Harry was looking over Mr Dyker's shoulder. "I'll do the darts," he said.

"Good at it, are you?" said Mr Dyker.

"Well, I won't be throwing them, will I?"

"Can I be on the breaking the crockery stall Dad?" shouted Ben.

"Now look," said Mr Dyker, "it's not fun and games this, you know. We've got to raise money for materials, timber, roofing and plumbing. The fête is dead serious – we've got to plan it properly."

"The fête should bring in a lot of money," said Jacky. "They raised five hundred pounds for the old people last year."

"I didn't see any of it," grumbled Harry, his nose twitching away.

"But you're not old," added Ben. An incredible smile flickered on to Harry's face and set up house there. He grinned from ear to ear.

"Well, I'll be blowed, that's the nicest thing that's been said to me for two years!" Everybody laughed.

Ben went to the door of the caravan and saw Mr Robson walking briskly towards them. The boys had started a game between themselves, in front of the caravan. Ben waved to Mr Robson and moved back inside again. "Mr Robson's coming," he called.

"OK," said Mr Dyker. "Get the lads here, we've got to set this up really strong."

Ben went to the doorway and yelled for the lads to come to the meeting. They broke off their game and jostled Mr Robson as he climbed up the slight slope to the steps. They all tried to crowd into the caravan, but a few of them had to sit outside and Soggy relayed everything to them. But as he didn't understand too much of what was going on, it came out a bit garbled.

Mr Robson took over the meeting and Mr Dyker read out his list of stalls.

"We'll rig a goal up," said Mr Dyker, "and have the crowd taking shots."

"Will Wayne be back in time?" asked Ben. Wayne was their brilliant goalkeeper, who had helped them so much in the Cup Final. He had had to leave right after the match and missed the dinner. His father was in the American Air Force and had been ordered to a base in Germany. Wayne had gone with him.

"He's coming back this weekend, he wrote to Jacky," replied Mr Dyker.

Ben nodded, "The team will be up to full strength," he said.

"Right," said Mr Dyker, "that's the goal sorted out."

"My Mam's making a cake, you know," said Jacky. "To guess the weight." Mr Robson ticked it off his list.

"I'm doing the darts," added Harry, pointing to the list.

"Are we having bowling for the pig?" shouted Soggy.

"You'll be sitting there all day," warned Nicky. "No one will want to win you, you know."

"Let's hope it's a fine day," added Mr Dyker smiling. "And everybody spends a lot of money."

It was a fine day. The sun shone like a life-long Brenton fan. Mr Robson couldn't believe the weather or the crowds flocking past his entrance table at the gate. "We'll have to send for some more tickets, Jacky."

Jacky nodded. "I'll fetch some when they thin out a bit."

She was at his side taking the money and handing out leaflets explaining the reason for the fête. Her face was flushed with the pushing and shoving from the people desperate to get in. Most of them wanted the secondhand clothes stall. The boys had been collecting hard. Soggy had donated his best suit, not because of the cause, but because he couldn't stand it. Unfortunately Molly had rescued it and put it safely back in Soggy's wardrobe.

Mr Dyker was on a tour of inspection. He stopped and watched Harry shouting the odds to the crowd at his dart stall. He was kept very busy dishing out the little goldfish in the plastic take-away bags. "Any three darts and you strike gold," he shouted at the top of his voice. He caught Mr Dyker's eye and winked broadly.

Mr Dyker put his hands on his hips and looked at the bustling fête and the nearly completed pitch beyond. Coloured balloons were tossing about, above the heads of the crowd, bunting had been stretched from stall to stall, flags were flying from the refreshment tent, where clouds of steam rose from the hole in the top, and a queue was already forming. He walked on to the crockery stall. Here a tiny housewife was doing terrible damage to a row of plates and saucers – the crowd loved it. A stranger kept paying her ten pence a go for her, laughing all over his face. His own wife was furious with him.

Mr Dyker walked on to the score-a-goal stall. Shambling Wayne and his freckles were between the sticks, while the young men of Brenton hammered shots at him. He was catlike, catching every ball. He waved to Mr Dyker. "It's great to be back, boss," he shouted. Mr

Dyker waved back at him. Niggle made Mr Dyker try a shot on the house and he put the ball away in the top right hand corner. Wayne shook his head. "Don't worry," shouted Mr Dyker, "I bent it."

"I think you nearly burst it," shouted Niggle, looking at the ball. Mr Dyker laughed and sauntered on. He watched the archery stand and saw Adrian's dad Greg, pulling the arrows out of the target. Just then a live arrow thudded into the board, two inches away from Greg's fingers. He turned slowly to look at the firing line. There stood Soggy, a limp bow in his hand and a limp expression on his face. Greg shuddered and walked towards Soggy. Mr Dyker moved away quickly, as he saw Greg point to the refreshment tent and shout, "I'd get over there, if I were you. They're sending up smoke signals – you'll be among friends there!" He didn't hear Soggy's reply as he walked back to the caravan, which was doubling as an office and first-aid post. He gazed again at the milling crowds, catching flashes of the Brenton boys in their blue and white tracksuits, running about, drumming up business. He caught Molly's eye on the second-hand clothes stall, and she waved at him; he waved back. The elderly first-aid lady, sitting in her canvas chair, squinted at the crowds above her knitting. "A bit slow today, isn't it?" she said.

"Is it?" asked Mr Dyker, slightly puzzled.

"Oh, yes," she went on. "I've usually had at least a nosebleed by now. You haven't got a headache, have you?"

Mr Dyker hid his smile. "No," he said. "I feel fine, absolutely fine." The old lady knitted on, in her crushed grey uniform, scanning the crowd for customers.

A couple of weeks later, Jacky and Harry were hurrying across a huge sportsfield, towards the football match. They were late, and Harry was fussing. "Rotten buses," he complained. Jacky was almost running to keep up with him. "They've started," he said, pointing to the match in progress. "I'm going to complain to the bus company."

Jacky said nothing. They were on the way to check on the Woodfield players for Mr Dyker. "Don't say anything to anybody Jacky. We don't want anyone to know we're here spying them out, yes?"

"I won't say a word, Harry."

"Right," said Harry as they reached the touchline. "We don't want to give the game away, do we?"

"No."

Harry lowered his voice. "As soon as we've played a few games, everybody will get to know us and we won't be able to size them up, but then again we'll have seen most of them play, won't we?"

"Yes, Harry," said Jacky, watching the game.

Harry pointed to a tall winger. "Eh, that lad looks good, moves well."

"Who?"

"Number seven," said Harry, concentrating on the action.

"How do we know which team is which?"

Harry saw the sense of Jacky's remark and, mentally kicking himself, said, "I'll ask someone." He turned to the nearest spectator who was dressed in a uniform. Probably a bus driver, thought Harry. "Eh, mate, which team is Woodfield?"

The man looked at Harry as if he were mad. "Neither," he said, after a long pause.

"What do you mean, neither?" said Harry.

The man, with one eye on the game and the other on this pest to his right said, "It's Bransome and Steverton, Woodfield is down the road." He looked at his watch, "Their match will just be over by now, they started early."

"Oh, lord," said Harry, his face showing his annoyance.

"Come to the wrong match have you?" asked the man.

"What do Woodfield play like?"

"Old women," replied the man. "Mind you they were runners-up last year, always in the top six."

Harry couldn't stand it any longer. "Come on Jacky," he shouted and started to run in the direction the man had indicated. Jacky ran after him and the man went on watching his game.

Once again they were running towards a football pitch where a game was in progress. As they got closer they heard a long piercing whistle, the referee had ended the match. As Harry and Jacky ran up the players began to stream off the pitch to the dressing rooms. Harry went straight up to a rather portly gentleman who was standing watching the teams come off the pitch, clapping his hands as the boys passed him. Harry touched him on the arm. "Who do you support mate, Woodfield?"

"Yes," said the man proudly.

"Who won?"

"Woodfield, of course," replied the man.

"How many?" asked Harry, getting agitated.

"Six, two," added the man pompously and he turned to go, but Harry stopped him.

"What's Woodfield like?" he asked, taking the man's arm. "I mean who are the danger men, what do they play? Four, four, two, or what? What's strongest, the defence or the attack?"

"You want to know a lot, don't you?" replied the man, trying to get away from Harry.

"No, no, just interested, just interested, that's all. We're er, from the local newspaper."

The man's eyes lit up. "The Woodfield Press?" he asked, raising his eyebrows.

Harry raised his as well. "Aye, that's right lad, Woodfield Press," and he took a battered notebook from his inside pocket, licked the stub of an old pencil and looked at the man. "What was your impression of the game? Hang on," he said pompously, "let's do this right, what's your name sir?"

The man preened himself and coughed gently, "Er, Arnold," he said, "Arnold Bingham," and he watched as Harry wrote the expert's name in his notebook.

"Now tell me your impression of the game. I want you to take us through every move, through every player."

Jacky had to turn away and stifle her laughter as Arnold, desperate to get into print with his knowledge of football, started to give Harry all Woodfield's secrets.

Harry's strategy worked beautifully. Two weeks later, on that pitch, Brenton played Woodfield. Brenton were all over them. For the first time, the boys were playing against bigger lads and better players than in their old League. But because of their hard work and superior training, they won easily. It felt great as they walked off after the final whistle. Mr Dyker was leading them to the dressing rooms and he was overjoyed with the team's first win of the season. "Four, one Harry, what a start! Your sussing them out worked well, Harry, how did you know their goalie hated ground shots?"

Harry smiled at Jacky as he said. "Saw it, didn't we Jacky? Saw

63

the way the lad went for the ball."

Mr Dyker patted Harry on the shoulder, "Well done Harry, well done."

"I didn't see the article Mr Leadbetter."

Harry's face fell, Arnold Bingham was standing in their path. "Ah, well," stuttered Harry, brushing past him. "It was er . . . in the er Southern editions only – space you know."

Arnold was clearly nonplussed. Then it dawned on him . . . Jacky smiled sweetly at him and he glared at them all the way to the dressing rooms.

"What was all that about?" asked Mr Dyker.

Harry pulled an uncomprehending face, "No idea boss, I've no idea," and he winked at Jacky, who threw her head back and laughed.

Mr Dyker shook his head, then clapping his hands he ran after the team. "Great lads," he shouted. "Great . . ."

On the way back, the landrover buzzed with the excited chatter of the winning team, as they did a post mortem on the game. "Nicky," shouted Mr Dyker. "We can still afford to tighten up a lot at the back. I want you inside men to get back in defence quicker, that's what the sprints are for. Wayne! You're still not thinking. Don't get rid of the ball too quickly. OK, you make fantastic saves, but don't give the ball away with your clearance, use Dolly more."

"Right on boss," shouted Wayne, grinning.

"How did I play, Mr Dyker?" Soggy's question was greeted with a huge moan.

"Great, Soggy," answered Mr Dyker. "Great, you all did. We hammered them, hammered them!" and he banged the horn button on his steering wheel, making all the cows raise their heads as the landrover swept through the country lanes, back to Brenton.

Later that night, Mr Dyker and Ben were lying in their bunks in the caravan, both still awake with the excitement. Mr Dyker had put the light out hours ago and it was he who broke the silence. "You played well today, son," he said gently.

"Thanks Dad," replied Ben, turning his head to look at his father.

"I mean it, you did well."

"Dolly's getting better, isn't he Dad?"

"Aye, they're all coming on," said Mr Dyker, then he paused. "Listen Ben, I can't single you out like the others. I mean, when I tell them how well they've done, I only seem to shout at your mistakes.

64

They may think it's favouritism, do you know what I mean?"

"You always tell me when we are alone."

"I know Ben, I know, but," Mr Dyker raised himself on one elbow, "sometimes I worry about you Ben. Don't ever drop your head because you get shouted at son, we can always talk it out."

"I know that," said Ben. "I'm not daft, Dad."

"When you're the number one striker," went on Mr Dyker, "they just expect miracles, every game. I know it happened to me, cheer the others like mad, all you get is groans when it goes wrong and abuse if you don't score in every game."

"It never bothers me, Dad."

Mr Dyker smiled in the darkness. "OK, you're growing up lad."

Ben grinned, "So are you," he said.

Mr Dyker chucked a cushion in the general direction of Ben. Silence descended again. Mr Dyker's cigarette glowed in the darkness.

"Ben."

"What?"

"What would you say if I got married again?"

"I'll have to have a new suit."

"I won't bother then."

"Is it Molly?"

"I'm saying nothing."

"Fancy having Soggy as a sister!"

"You mean a brother, don't you?"

"I know what I mean," said Ben. "Goodnight Dad."

"Goodnight, son."

"Don't forget to put your fag out."

"I'll have you in a minute," said Mr Dyker, but Ben was too sleepy to hear.

Seven

A huge sledge hammer whistled through the air, nearly taking Soggy's head with it, forcing the tent peg into the ground. Mr Baker set himself up for another swing to fix the peg home. "Stand back a bit lad," he said, and Soggy retreated in front of the impending hammer blow. The peg quivered and nearly split, as it was driven in hard. Mr Baker wiped the sweat from his forehead and nodded at the quivering peg. "That won't shift."

"I think you went in for a bit of overkill there," said Soggy, warily.

Mr Baker looked at him and then turned to look up at the huge marquee which the shattered peg was helping to keep upright. "Suppose we have a storm?" he thundered. "That tent would lift straight out of the ground without proper fixing."

Soggy shaded his eyes and looked up at the twin towers of the huge tent. Bunting was flying between them and flags were fluttering from the top of the main poles. Pennants had been fixed to the heavy guy lines as well, and signs had been lashed to some of them, to indicate the direction of the refreshments, temporary toilets, and the changing areas for visitors and home team. The whole scene was bustling with overworked dads, scrambling about with last-minute jobs to get the tent and the pitch ready for the team's first home game.

Soggy had been annoying everyone almost since dawn, track suit on, kit in his bag over his shoulder. Mr Baker looked at him, "Eh, you're going to take root here. You've been waiting hours now."

"I know," said Soggy, proudly. "It's our first home game, I can't believe it. Our first home game," he repeated, looking at the frenzied activity and rocking on his heels.

"You'd better win, that's all," replied Mr Baker, lifting the huge sledge hammer onto his shoulder.

"Well, we won our first two away matches, Woodfield and Hatton, four, one and two, nil," shouted Soggy.

"Two nil? You're slipping aren't you?" scoffed Dolly's dad.

"No!" said Soggy firmly. "We got in front and bottled the game up, on instructions from Mr Dyker."

"Oh, aye," said Mr Baker, his eyes twinkling. "Pull the other one."

"We play to a formula," said Soggy doggedly. "Every game is different."

"Oh, yes, what's going to happen to this one then?"

"I don't know, he hasn't told us yet."

"Oh, aye."

"We have a pre-match chat you see."

"You mean like Don Revie and his lot?" asked Mr Baker, with his tongue in his cheek.

"Something like that," agreed Soggy. "Only Mr Dyker's much better." He fixed Mr Baker with a withering stare, "He knows what he's talking about."

"Oh," he said, firmly put in his place. "I see, well good luck anyway," and he moved on to mutilate the next peg.

"Oh, you don't need luck," shouted Soggy, "only application!" Mr Baker nearly dropped the hammer on his foot. "And skill! And unselfish running! And hard tackling!" At that Mr Baker did drop the hammer on his foot.

"Shut up," he yelled, as he swiped at the innocent peg and it split from top to bottom.

 On their way to the pitch, Mark and Nicky were pacing each other on their bikes. They were both wearing track suits and had the inevitable football bags slung over their shoulders. They were keyed up and disdainful of the slight traffic, as they weaved and bobbed down the High Street, using the pavement when they ran out of road. Wheel to wheel they kept up a continuous nervous chatter. "Our first home game," shouted Mark.

"You've said that four times," said Nicky.

Mark looked at him. "Feel sharp Nick?"

"Don't I always."

They pedalled on. Mark chose to sit up and ride without hands and Nicky followed suit. "What did Harry and his 'snooping out' say about this lot?" asked Mark.

"Denton? Big-headed Denton?" replied Nick. Mark nodded. "Very posh," said Nicky, "very posh. All far-back accents, you know, 'hammer-freds' – you know, hammer-fred we've just scored. Hammer-fred we're too good for you. Hammer-fred you've lahrst . . . hah . . . hah . . . hah. . ."

Mark dropped his hands down on to his handlebars to oblige a passing lorry driver and said, "Hammer-fred we'll knock hell out of them then."

"Hammer-fred you're right," answered Nicky, steering himself out of trouble round a slow-moving Mini.

As the boys joined up again, Mark shouted, "What are you doing tomorrow Nick?"

Nicky pulled a face. "Homework and nothing really."

"Want to come shooting with us? My dad asked me to invite you."

Nicky's face creased into a grin, "Great! What time?"

"Ten o'clock," replied Mark, and waved at a little girl pulling faces at them from the back seat of a car.

"Right," shouted Nicky, and they raced on to the pitch.

As the scattered Brenton team fussed and preened itself and made ready for their first home match, the enemy or opposition was having trouble.

They were in convoy, a splendid black Rolls Royce and a sturdy brown Range Rover, gliding up and down the sleepy lanes around Brenton, trying to home in on the newly completed pitch. Finally the Rolls hissed to a stop and the driver, wearing a snow-white sheepskin jacket, hissed out and went to confer with his companion. They spread a large map over the bonnet of the Range Rover and boiled over. Noel, the Rolls owner, driver and father of two of the Denton players, poked the map with his gloved hand. "In the silly fool's letter, he said turn right at that 'T' junction. Well we did that, didn't we Ronnie?"

"We certainly did," replied Ronnie.

"I can't see anything marked here, can you Ronnie?"

"I most certainly can't."

The two cars had disgorged the passengers. They sauntered round, stretching and yawning in complete boredom, all in very fetching matching track suits. Noel folded up the map and, very fed up now, waved it towards a crossroads further on. "Oh, let's try down there," he said.

Ronnie nodded. "Can't do any harm," he agreed.

"Who is this team anyway, Ronnie?"

68

"Brenton," answered Ronnie. "They did the double in the Lord Beaker League last year."

"Did they?" murmured Noel, pursing his lips.

"Yes, that's how they qualified for the County."

"Hmmm, interesting," muttered Noel, "interesting." He lifted his head and spoke crisply to the sauntering Denton team. "Sorry about this, chaps, can't seem to find the venue. Please bear with us. Let's get back on board, shall we?" The lads clambered back into their magnificent chariots.

Back at the Brenton pitch, Mr Dyker had gathered the first team in front of the entrance to the borrowed marquee. He was giving them his pre-match chat and the lads were listening with their full attention. Molly was inside the huge entrance, polishing and playing with the large tea urn, on loan with the tent. She treated it as though it was alive, jumping every time it gurgled and hissed. Mr Dyker's voice came drifting through from outside.

"We don't know much about this team," he said, "so just keep it tight. Help one another, run for one another. I don't want to see anybody standing still, understand?" he bellowed. Molly jumped and Mr Dyker went on. "Run lads, run the whole sixty minutes, yes?"

"Yes!" they all chorused back. Soggy felt like running round the pitch then and there. Niggle held him back.

Mr Dyker lowered his voice. "Listen lads, listen very hard. I don't want any trouble with this team," he looked about him, and waved at the tent. "We are supposed to have showers and toilets and proper dressing rooms, so no aggro, yes?"

"Yes, Mr Dyker," they all shouted.

Soggy pointed to the two tents away from the main one. "We have got proper toilets over there," he said. "I think they're smashing."

"Soggy!" shouted Nicky.

"I do," insisted Soggy. "I've used them twice, they're great."

Bomber raised his head, "I'm not going in there then."

Mr Dyker ignored them. "Just play your game," he said. "Let's hope they don't complain about the 'facilities'."

Mark frowned. "Could they really have us thrown out of the League, Mr Dyker?"

Mr Dyker nodded. "If they wanted to be awkward, yes. It's all down in the rules and regulations, we were sent a copy. It's in the lap of the gods. Let's hope they accept what we have to offer."

The boys looked at each other. Nicky spoke for them all.

"We'll keep our fingers crossed," he said.

"I still think they're smashing toilets," said Soggy.

Wayne picked him up and threw him to Dolly. Mr Dyker went on with his pre-match instructions.

 The expensive visiting convoy had found the correct lane but hadn't sighted the ground yet. They sighted Harry instead, striding along with his stomach on fire in anticipation of the big match. The Rolls glided alongside him and Noel leaned out of the window. "Tell me, my man," he shouted.

"Yes?" shouted Harry, in alarm. He hadn't heard the car come up behind him.

Noel went on, "Do you know where the . . ." he turned back into the car. "What's the infernal name again?" he asked the passengers.

"Brenton, boring Brenton," they chanted back at him.

Noel smiled sweetly at Harry. "Do you know where the Brenton Boys' football pitch might be located?"

Harry nodded, "Oh, aye."

"Is it far from here?" asked Noel.

Harry shook his head, sizing up the lads in the car. "No, it's not far at all."

Noel smiled again, "Could you direct us?"

"I can do better than that, I'm going there myself. I'll show you if you like."

"Oh," said Noel, not quite sure. "I see, well, I suppose you'd better get in."

Harry nipped round to the front seat, passenger side, and squeezed alongside the young athlete sitting there. "Play a bit, do you?" he asked, looking at him. The lad nodded. "Brenton are terriers," Harry went on, widening his eyes as though the lad was heading for a street accident. "You stand no chance son, no chance whatsoever, no chance at all! You go left here and follow the road round." This last bit was directed at Noel whose mouth dropped open as he listened. Harry sank back into the seat and enjoyed the ride, painting more horrors for the visitors.

Mr Dyker looked at his watch. "They're late," he said.

70

"Shall I take a look down to the dual carriageway?" asked Mr Robson.

Mr Dyker shook his head. "No, we'll give them another few minutes."

The team were in their strip and chewing hard on the gum Mr Robson had shared out. Niggle was retying his laces again, and the others were pushing a ball about. Nicky had jumped to head the ball, but he caught it instead and shouted, "Oh, no! Will you look at that!"

The others followed his gaze and saw the Rolls and Range Rover sweep into the field, with Harry, as large as life, waving his arms and directing the convoy from the front seat. The Rolls pulled up in front of Mr Dyker and Noel leaned out. "Where's the car park, old chap?" he asked. Harry had got out and slammed the door.

"You'll be all right there," replied Mr Dyker, biting his lip.

Noel gazed at the marquee. "Oh, what a pretty tent, having a fête?"

The Brenton lads watched as the opposition dismounted from the two imposing cars, and their eyebrows shot up as they saw the huge wicker basket taken out of the Rolls' boot.

"What have you got in there," shouted Harry, "sandwiches?"

Noel smiled sweetly at him. "Just our kit," he said. "Where do we change, old chap?"

"In here with us," said Soggy, pointing to the pretty tent.

Ronnie pulled a face. "Oh, do we?" he asked.

Soggy nodded. "And the toilets are over there," he said pointing. "They're smashing."

Noel looked stunned. "Thank you, you're very kind," he muttered and led the way into the tent, nodding at Molly as though she was being inspected. He shouted to Mr Dyker, over his shoulder, "And no showers I take it? That's a bore."

Mr Dyker looked at Mr Robson and they both raised their eyebrows at each other as they followed their own team inside the tent.

The first half was played out according to Mr Dyker's instructions. The Brenton lads held Denton very well. Wayne had had nothing to do in goal. Ben had laid the ball off instead of going on one of his runs. Mark and Nicky soon got the Denton midfield sorted out. The boys played very well together, long searching passes, one-twos with each other, switching it from wing to wing. Niggle and Dolly and Bomber were finding each other without looking. It had been very pretty football, but no goals.

As the two teams came off at half-time, Noel walked alongside Mr Dyker. "Well, nil, nil," he said. "You've held us very well, very useful team you have Dyker, very useful. Your finishing is a bit slack, if you don't mind me saying so, but you show a lot of promise." He looked across at Mr Dyker. "We have maximum points so far, you know. Won our first three games, no problems." Noel put his hands behind his back and dropped his voice. "I must say old son, your dressing room arrangements are a little off. Quite a surprise!"

Mr Dyker flannelled a smile at him. "Yes, well, we're in the process of building a new clubhouse." He gestured to the unfinished building behind the marquee.

"Really? Really?" said Noel. "Did the League know about your predicament?"

Mr Dyker pretended ignorance. "Oh, do they have to?"

"Oh, yes," chimed in Ronnie. "They must come up to standard, you know. Can't have the lads changing in a field, can we?"

"No I suppose not," said Mr Dyker.

"It won't do them any harm," shouted Harry, bringing up the rear of the party.

Noel turned to him. "That's not the point, is it," he said waspishly.

"God knows," said Harry, under his breath.

The two rival factions entered their curtained-off dressing areas and supped the tea Molly had placed there. Mr Dyker waved the boys to him. Soggy was on the ground, with his ear to the bottom of the canvas divider, listening to the Denton team on the other side.

Mark whispered to Mr Dyker. "We've got them cold now, we're playing with them. Can we start scoring?"

Mr Dyker shook his head sadly. "You're doing great lads, great, only Harry and I know you're pulling your shots."

Nicky rubbed the back of his neck. "It's quite a strain, Mr Dyker."

"I know lads, I know," he said. He made them sit on the floor, then looked at their flushed faces, Brenton were all expectation – eager to thrash this cocky side, eager to blood their new pitch with a good home win. He swallowed and shook his head. "Listen kids," he said, "you're about to have your first defeat."

The boys couldn't believe him, some of them moaned and groaned. "Why? Why?" "We've got them stone cold." "What do you mean, Mr Dyker?"

Mr Dyker sank on to his haunches, his elbows on his knees. "Let them in lads."

"*Let them in?*" shouted Dolly.

"Shush!" said Mr Dyker, pointing to the partition, his finger to his lips. "Let them in Dolly, let them get a goal."

Dolly shook his head, "Why? Why did you tell us to hold them?"

Mr Dyker looked round at their incredulous faces and answered: "Politics lads, politics. If we beat this lot, think! They'll get grotty and complain about our pitch, the tent, the lack of showers, everything! Let them beat us, they'll go away happy and we stay in the League, OK?"

The boys wouldn't believe what they were hearing. "Ah, come off it, Mr Dyker, it's not fair, it's our first home match!" said Bomber.

Mr Dyker looked kindly at him. "It'll be your last if you don't do as I say. Play to the plan, right?"

The boys dropped their heads. "Right!" they answered, sullenly.

Soggy came creeping up to them. "Eh, they're all moaning about the tea, the bucket of water for washing, the pitch, everything. That posh feller's telling them not to let it put them off."

Mr Dyker opened up his arms wide to his team at this confirmation. "Let them in," he said again, "it's only one game. When you've got your clubhouse and showers, you can hammer them. Do as I say lads, please?" He clapped his hands together. "Some you have to lose, yes?"

They nodded their heads but they didn't believe what he was asking them to do. "OK boss," Mark answered for them. Ben looked sick.

When the referee blew his whistle, Brenton got possession easily. Niggle pushed it to Nicky and he was off, haring down the wing. He crossed it to Mark who collected it easily and shot it at their goalkeeper. Mr Dyker's heart missed a beat. The lad fumbled it and nearly gave a goal away. From the clearance, Dolly allowed the Denton winger to bustle past him. Niggle slowed to a walk in the middle and left their centre forward alone to collect the cross and score. Wayne could have saved it even then, but his frantic dive and pretended anguish convinced even Soggy, who should have known what was going on. Mr Dyker smiled bitterly. He looked at Harry and nodded at Wayne. "He deserves an oscar for that. He had it covered all the way, even though we let their lad have a clear shot." Harry shook his head.

On the field Ben trotted up to Mark. "OK," he said, "some we have to lose, but it's only going to be one goal, all right? Let's give them a lesson in bad finishing." Mark nodded at him.

They tore through Denton's defence and Ben finished the exercise with a rugby kick over the bar. Harry applauded, until he saw Noel watching him.

"Nice try," shouted Noel.

Harry smiled back and snarled between gritted teeth. "Just you wait, just you wait . . ."

Brenton acted like heroes. Every lad fell over himself, miss-kicked, got himself off side, handled the ball. Dolly nearly got himself booked, but they did what Mr Dyker asked them to do, all except Soggy, who was day-dreaming at the boredom of it all. He fastened on a loose ball and beat off two tackles. One of them was Niggle, who knew by the look in Soggy's eyes he'd forgotten Mr Dyker's instructions. Soggy ploughed on down the middle, sent the goalie the wrong way and scored, and immediately realised with horror, what he'd done. He chased after the referee, protesting he was off side by a mile, and he'd handled it as well. "Nonsense," the referee shouted at him. "Nonsense lad, it was a good goal."

Soggy's eyes rolled to the back of his head as the rest of the team glared at him. The referee blew time and Brenton dragged itself off the pitch. Soggy walked off alone.

Later, the team and Mr Dyker were seeing the visitors off and holding their breath. They watched them place the kit in the back of the Rolls, standing in a silent group, as the lofty Denton players took up their seats in the two cars. Ronnie climbed into his car and Noel turned to Mr Dyker. He offered his hand. "Good game, good game," said Noel. "Useful draw for us, you did well."

Mr Dyker smiled and gestured to the tent behind him. "I'm sorry about the . . ."

Noel broke in on him. "Don't mention it, don't mention it. Let's hope next time we come, your building will be more advanced."

Mr Dyker pumped his hand with relief. "Yes," he agreed. "Let's hope so."

Noel looked about him then smiled at the Brenton lads, waved and climbed into his car. With, "Well, goodbye then, see you soon," he was gone. The boys waved after him, until the convoy turned out of the field.

Mr Dyker stopped waving, the lads stopped waving, they turned and looked at Soggy. Mr Dyker dropped his arm and shouted. "Soggy!"

"What boss?"

"I'll give you what boss!" said Mr Dyker. "What do you mean by scoring?"

"Well, er . . ." started Soggy. "Er, I forgot."

"You clot!" shouted Mr Dyker. "What did I tell you?"

Mark answered for all of them. "Let's get him."

"Yes," echoed Nicky. "Let's get him."

Niggle shouted. "Let me have him, I'm the one who tackled him, the lunatic."

Soggy dropped his bag and started to run, the lads ran after him. Molly came out with a tray of tea. They all drank and watched as Soggy was caught and thrown in the air, up and down. They could hear a chant coming from the group of lads? "What are you?" they cried in unison.

"I'm a bit forgetful at times, that's all," shouted Soggy. But he was giggling and they heard him add: "I'm the first one to score on our home pitch." At that they threw him even higher.

Mr Dyker turned to Molly, "You know, this is the best cup of tea I've ever tasted, Molly."

Eight

The early morning mist was drifting across the pitch. A few wood pigeons whirred about, looking for breakfast. The weak sun was promising a dry day, and the windows of the caravan were misted up on the inside. Powerful snores reverberated from the caravan, Mr Dyker's, of course. It was Saturday, match day, Cup Match day. Brenton's first, and everyone was sleeping, all except Brian Woodgate. He had left his two-stroke motor bike by the entrance gate and was getting the bottoms of his trousers soaking wet with dew as he ran through the long grass towards the caravan. He shouted as he got nearer, "Dyker! Dyker! Ben. Ben are you awake?" The snores continued. He leaned on the caravan door to get his breath back, then pounded on it with his fist. He turned and looked at the completed clubhouse in the far distance. New paint flashing in the sunshine. New roof casting a new shadow over the car park. He looked at it with pride, then remembering his mission, pounded on the door again. Mr Dyker opened the door, stretching and yawning in his pyjamas. "What's the rush?" he asked.

"I'm sorry to get you out of bed at this hour, Mr Dyker. I've got some bad news I'm afraid."

Mr Dyker looked at his visitor. "Oh," he said, "what's that?"

"Two of your lads won't be able to play in the Cup Match today."

"What do you mean?" asked Mr Dyker.

Mr Woodgate licked his lips and said, "There's been a car accident."

"What?"

"Who is it?" shouted Ben, jumping out of his bunk and joining his father at the door.

"Cheddar and Ian," went on Mr Woodgate, sadly. "They're not hurt bad. They're at home in bed, cuts and bruises. They've both got stitches, they can't move."

76

Ben was still half asleep. "What happened?" he asked.

Mr Woodgate told him. "They were coming home last night, from swimming. You know Cheddar's father takes them on a Friday night, and they skidded on some mud into a gate on Jennings farm. The car's in a state as well, it's still there. They've pushed it onto the verge, it's a write-off."

Mr Dyker found his temper rising, "Never mind the car, what about our Cup Match?" he roared.

"You'll be two short, I'm afraid," Mr Woodgate said, backing away slightly. "Cheddar's mum phoned me and asked me to let you know. She's looking after her husband."

"Was he driving?" asked Mr Dyker.

Mr Woodgate nodded. "Yes, he's done a few ribs in as well, and his no claims bonus. He's only had the car a few weeks. They were going abroad in it – I think the chassis's twisted myself – he snapped the gatepost off, clean as a whistle."

Mr Dyker collapsed onto his bunk, his head in his hands. "That's great that is, just great."

Ben and Mr Woodgate looked at each other. "We can't play ten men, can we Dad?" asked Ben.

Mr Dyker raised his head and looked at them both. "We'll be knocked out of the Cup in the first round, wouldn't you just know it," he said bitterly, and brought his fist down on the tiny dining table, making the breakfast things jump.

Ben rescued a couple of plates as they threatened to drop on to the floor. Mr Woodgate poked his head into the caravan, licking his lips nervously. "Er, Mrs Cheddar asked me to let you know – you know."

Mr Dyker touched him on the shoulder. "Thanks," he said. "I appreciate it."

'I'll be getting along then. Will you be playing this afternoon?"

Mr Dyker shook his head. Ben reached out to steady the table in case. "I don't know yet," sighed Mr Dyker. "We'll have to do something, we just can't concede the match."

Ben jumped in. "We can hold anyone with ten men, Dad."

"Don't bank on it. Ian keeps that midfield together."

Mr Woodgate looked down at his wet shoes and thought it was time to go. "You're opening the new clubhouse today, aren't you?"

Ben answered for his father. "Yes, it's ready."

Niggle's dad smiled sadly. "Well, I'll come along anyway for that, so good luck. Play like blazes Ben."

"Thanks for letting us know," shouted Mr Dyker.

"Not at all," said Mr Woodgate, by now half-way down the field. "Goodbye."

Ben shouted, "Goodbye," and waved, then shut the door.

Mr Dyker rubbed his unshaven chin and looked at Ben. "I'm not awake yet, are you?" he asked.

"No."

Mr Dyker shook his head and peeled off his pyjama jacket, "What a way to start the day," he said. "Let's hope nothing else goes wrong!"

Down in the dip on the other side of the clubhouse, Harry was giving Bob a lecture on how to behave in the vicinity of the new building. "I don't want you cocking your leg up on that now," he said, waving his finger at Bob and the new wall of the clubhouse. "It's taken a lot of effort, that place and you will show it proper respect. So think on what I'm telling you. I won't be able to help you if any of the lads catch you. So get it into your head now, no snapping at the boys' legs while they're playing, not on our side anyway, and no doing your doings either." Bob cocked his ears at him. "Never mind looking at me like that, just you do as you are told, understand?" Bob wagged his tail. Harry wandered round to the front of the new building and was immediately incensed by what he saw.

A thin little man in a black overcoat and hat was pinning a notice to the magnificent double doors. Harry felt the colour rising on the back of his neck. Bob must have sensed something was not quite right, as he started to growl softly. Harry couldn't speak at first, his rage wouldn't let him, he bristled and Bob raised his hackles. Finally he found his voice. "Eh!" he shouted, "what do you think you are doing? Those doors have just been varnished. You can't go round sticking things on like that, take it off, whatever it is!"

The little man was startled. "Sorry mate," he said. "I'm just doing my job."

Harry was almost dancing with rage. "What's that you're putting up?"

The man pompously finished tacking the sheet of paper to the door, then turned to Harry. "I am putting up a Charging Order," he said. "Someone hasn't been paying his bills."

Harry was flabbergasted. "The only bill we owe," he shouted, "is the plumber's. That's Mr Stanmore, and he's agreed to wait."

The little man shook his head. "I think you'll find Mr Stanmore has gone bankrupt, and his main creditor is out for blood. This is the first of many." The little man waved a sheaf of official-looking forms at Harry and then thrust them back into his battered briefcase.

"What does it mean?" asked Harry, fear and worry mounting.

The little man smiled at him. "Pay up, or you'll lose whatever's in there," he said, nodding at the clubhouse. "The stuff will be seized and sold."

"Seized and sold?" repeated Harry. "Listen, we don't want any trouble today, it's our first Cup Match."

"Don't talk to me mate," said the little man.

"Mr Stanmore said he'd wait!" said Harry pressing on.

The little man shook his head. "That's how he got into trouble in the first place," he said, smiling.

Harry tried a new tack. "How much is it?" he asked.

The man took out a well-thumbed small notebook and flicked the pages. He found what he was looking for. "Two hundred and fifty," he said. "Not much, when you come to think about it."

Harry's eyes sparkled. "I've got some money in the Building Society."

"That's not doing me much good, is it?" said the little man.

Harry went on. "I can't get my hands on it until Monday, can I?"

The little man thought for a while, and made a few notes in his book. At last he turned to Harry. "I'll ring the office," he said. "I'll be back later on. I may be able to get you to sign something, OK?"

Harry shook his head. "OK," he echoed.

The little man fastened his overcoat and snapped his briefcase shut. With a final tap to the large fixing pins of the Charging Order, he smiled at Harry and walked away.

Harry watched him go, and as he turned out of the gate, he looked down at Bob. "That's a nice start, isn't it? Eh? All we need on a Cup Day a bit of worry, a bit of bother to throw us off balance. It's an important match this, you know." He pulled on the lead, jerking Bob's head round. "Look at me when I'm talking to you," shouted Harry. Bob's tail went between his legs.

 Mr Dyker had shaved and was going through the motions of eating his breakfast with Ben but neither of them felt like food at that moment. There was a knock at the door. "More trouble?" said Mr Dyker, as Ben rose to open it. Mark, Nick and Wayne stood there in an embarrassed group.

"Hey, Mr Dyker," shouted Wayne, "have you heard about Ian and Cheddar?"

Mr Dyker nodded his head "Yes, first thing this morning," he grunted.

"What are we going to do?" asked Mark. The boys crowded into the tiny caravan and sat on the bunks, all tidy now as Ben had been busy. "Listen," he said, "with the sub we've got ten men. If we bring anyone else in it'll just destroy the rhythm, so why don't we . . ."

Mr Dyker cut in on him. "Ben reckons we can hold them with ten men."

Mark agreed. "Of course we can," he said, "easy!"

"It's better than not playing," said Nicky.

"Can't we just postpone it?" asked Wayne.

Mr Dyker shook his head. "Can't be done, can't be done, too late. Now we've got the facilities, we haven't got the players." He paused and looked round at the worried faces. "We're not jinxed are we?"

Nicky quickly said, "Not on your life, Mr Dyker."

"We could go for a draw," said Mark. "Hold them like we did last time."

Mr Dyker pushed his chair back and stood up, the boys stood up as well. "Come on, let's get down to the clubhouse and see what's what. We can get some training in at least."

They all left the caravan. Ben locked the door and trotted after them. He felt sick, he knew his father was close to packing the whole thing in. Why did Cheddar and Ian have to go swimming, he asked himself? Why couldn't they have missed it for one week? He caught the others up and the group walked on in silence. For once there didn't seem to be anything to say. Ben could just see Soggy and Jacky with a few others at the entrance to the clubhouse. He waved to Soggy and Soggy waved back. Nicky tried a joke, "At least Soggy's right arm is still working," he said. No one laughed, they walked on in silence.

As they approached the building, they heard Soggy shout, "Eh, Mr Dyker, have you heard?"

Mr Dyker nodded. "Yes, Sogg," he said. "First thing this morning."

"It's so unfair," said Jacky, "especially on our first Cup Match."

"Harry's got some money in the Building Society," added Soggy. The others did not understand Soggy at all.

"What's he going to do with it," asked Ben, "bribe the other team?"

"No," said Soggy doggedly. "Pay for the plumbing."

Mr Dyker pricked his ears up. "What did you say – do what for the plumbing?"

Soggy looked at them all, doubt written all over his face. "You said you knew!" he said accusingly.

"About Ian and Cheddar," said Ben.

"What about Ian and Cheddar?" asked Soggy, completely lost.

Mr Dyker tried to resolve it. "Soggy," he said, taking his arm, "very slowly, as slowly as you like, tell me what Harry said to you."

Soggy wriggled about and looked at the other boys, his face went red. "Oh, well, er – he's er, gone to get some money to . . . er . . . because the piping and that . . . er . . . isn't paid for and er . . . eh, what's happened to Ian and Cheddar, have they been kidnapped?"

Ben put him out of his misery. "They've been in a car accident."

"They can't drive!" said Soggy.

Mr Dyker gave up and turned to Jacky. "What's he on about Jacky?" he asked.

Jacky brought them up to date. They had got up early and wandered to the ground to have a look at the clubhouse. They had seen Harry and he had told them a man had been there saying he was going to seize all the belongings in the clubhouse, because Mr Stanmore's bill hadn't been paid.

Mr Dyker sank down on to the wooden steps leading up to the veranda of the clubhouse. "Oh, no," he said, "that's all we need."

"Harry said not to worry," offered Jacky.

"He's going to play midfield for us, is he?" asked Mr Dyker.

Jacky dropped her head. "No," she said quietly. "I think he

81

meant not to worry about the money."

Mr Dyker was ashamed. "Sorry Jacky, I didn't mean to snap your head off."

"That's all right, Mr Dyker," said Soggy. Jacky glared at him.

Mr Dyker stood up. "Come on you lot," he shouted. "Whatever happens, we'll get some training in." He opened the front doors and Nicky ran in and picked up the practice ball. The rest of the lads followed him on to the practice area. Mr Dyker sat in the home team's dressing room, trying to sort things out. He heard hurried footsteps on the wooden veranda. They came nearer, first into the clubhouse and then into the dressing room.

"What are you going to do?" Mr Dyker looked up to see Mr Robson standing there, looking very agitated.

"Have a little think," answered Mr Dyker.

Mr Robson paced up and down. "We're still having the official opening, aren't we?"

"Oh, yes, we'll open the club. Whether we play a match or not is debatable at the moment."

Mr Robson had heard about Harry's visitor. "What about this Court Order," he said.

Mr Dyker managed a brief smile. "Harry's told me not to worry."

"And?" said Mr Robson.

Mr Dyker clapped his hands together. "What do you think?"

Mr Robson paced harder. "Murder will be done today if this place isn't open on time. Everybody's worked so hard."

"We must keep calm," said Mr Dyker.

Mr Robson looked at his watch and stopped pacing. He drew a large breath and said, "Mr Eckersley will be here at two pm to cut the ribbon. I've managed to get ribbon in the club's colours. He'll give a short speech and then we're off."

Mr Dyker looked at him. "OK," he said finally.

Mr Robson started his pacing again. "I'll start to check everything now. Are you all right?"

Mr Dyker nodded his head. "Yes," he said, "I'm fine, fine, fine . . ."

Outside, lapping the pitch, the team had worked up a little sweat. They were doing a gentle jog and having a natter at the same time. "*I've* played with stitches in my head," shouted Soggy.

"Yes," agreed Nicky, "and look what it did for you."

"I think they should turn out," argued Soggy.

"The doctor won't allow them, you daft nit," chimed in Mark.

Soggy threw his head back, "What do doctors know?" he challenged. The boys ran on.

Back in the dressing room, Mr Dyker heard soft footsteps, and looking up he saw that Jacky had entered the room. She stared at Mr Dyker and he smiled at her. "Mr Dyker," said Jacky.

"Hello, Jacky."

"Mr Dyker, we do have an extra player," she went on.

Mr Dyker's face lit up. "Someone I don't know about?" he asked. "Someone who's turned out for us before?"

"Yes," said Jacky, nodding her head.

"Tell me more," said Mr Dyker. "It'll solve one of our problems anyway."

Later that afternoon, all the parents, with the team and their fans, gathered outside the new clubhouse. It was nearly two o'clock and the official opening was about to be performed. All eyes were straining towards the gate to catch sight of Mr Eckersley's car. A small table had been placed on the veranda, in front of the ribbon, stretching across the entrance. The Cup and Shield which the boys had won in their old League, were standing there, sparkling in the sunshine. Mr Robson looked about him, checked his watch and grimaced at Mr Dyker. "We're going to be late," he said.

Harry was in the crowd nervously looking about. He jumped as a cheer went up. It wasn't Mr Eckersley, it was the Denton team in their splendid convoy. Noel and Ronnie steered their team safely into the new car park and disembarked for the Cup Match with Brenton. The ground was buzzing with excitement, as Noel approached Mr Dyker. "Hello, Dyker," he shouted. "What a turnout! I'm afraid we're going to beat you, old chap. We always have a good run in the Cup. I say," Noel stopped in his tracks and leaned back in admiration. "I say, is that your new clubhouse? What an improvement on our last visit, eh? What? Come on Ronnie, mustn't hold up the ceremony." They struggled into the clubhouse, manhandling the wicker basket under the line of ribbon, with their team following.

Nicky nodded at them as they disappeared and looked at Ben. "Every time we play this team we have two strikes against us."

"Relax," said Ben. "Relax, we can beat them with ten men easy, no problem, can't we Sogg?"

"Well," said Soggy, "I scored against them on my own."

Mark shoved him. "If your head gets any bigger, Soggy, you'll have to live in a barn."

"They don't scare me," added Soggy, glaring at the clubhouse. "I'm a class player."

Ben pounded him on the back. "That's the way, Sogg, hammer them."

Soggy glowed.

Mr Eckersley arrived and apologised for being late. Everyone shook hands. Mr Robson called for silence. "Ladies and gentlemen, please." The chatter and skylarking went on. "Ladies and gentlemen, can I have your attention, *please*?"

Soggy spotted Mr Robson's problem and leant inside the Rolls and gave a long blast on the horn. There was silence as everyone looked at Soggy. He smiled and gestured to Mr Robson. The crowd dutifully turned and gave their attention. "Thank you Soggy," said Mr Robson. "Ladies and gentlemen," he went on. "You all know what a splendid day this is for Brenton. Without more ado, I'd like to hand you over to Mr Eckersley, who very kindly has offered to open our new clubhouse." There was long applause and cheering. Mr Eckersley held his hands up to calm them down. Harry was cheering with the rest, when he caught sight of the little man, who had caused so much upset that morning with his Charge Order. Harry went over and stood in front of him, as he tried to barge through the crowd.

"Eh!" cried the little man. "Who's taken down my Charge Order?"

"I did," said Harry, showing him the piece of paper.

The man bristled. "You're not allowed to do that," he shouted.

Harry placed his hand on the man's sleeve. "Can't we discuss this over a beer?" he said. "We don't want any fuss, do we?"

The little man looked at Harry and cleared his throat. "You're prepared to pay the amount out of your funds in your Building Society?" he asked.

"That is what I said," agreed Harry.

"You'll have to sign an undertaking," threatened the little man.

"You're not burying me, are you?" asked Harry, his eyes gleaming.

"No! It's a contract."

84

Harry put his hands over his ears. "Come on to the Plough," he shouted. "I can't hear myself speak here."

The little man nodded and left, with many a backward glance to the crowd milling round the clubhouse.

Mr Eckersley finally got some sort of order and quiet from the excited crowd. His good-natured face creased into a grin as he waved the large pair of scissors about. "Ladies and gentlemen," began Mr Eckersley, "the last time we all met was a very sad occasion. I had to tell the boys their pitch had been taken away from them for good. We all thought football in Brenton had come to an end, but . . . but . . . it was not to be." He gestured with the scissors to his left. "Mr Robson here," he went on, "and you stalwarts," he gestured to the dads in the crowd.

"I'm labour!" shouted a wag and got a laugh.

"You stalwarts," Mr Eckersley went on, "wouldn't take the news lying down, and with muscle, enterprise, long hours, and damned hard work, you've produced what we see here today." Mr Eckersley turned and looked at the building. "A splendid clubhouse," he thundered, "a splendid pitch, a splendid achievement."

Nicky shouted. "The team's not bad either!" and everybody laughed.

Mr Eckersley twinkled at Nicky and went on. "It is now my pleasant duty to cut the ribbon and declare this new Brenton Boys' Football Club and Ground, officially open, and welcome home these hard-won trophies." He picked up the Cup and showed it to the crowd, who cheered and shouted, then he slowly cut the ribbon. The two ends fell away and there was silence for a while, then long, happy applause and cheering, which must have frightened the Denton players inside. Mr Robson put his hands in the air to get attention again.

"Ladies and gentlemen, we hope you will all stay on for the boys' match and give them your support." The cheering answered this request. Mr Robson and Mr Dyker shook hands and waved at the crowd.

In the Plough bar, Harry approached the little man with two foaming pints. "I'm not a hard man, you know," he said. "I've got kids of my own."

Harry thrust the pint at him. "Have another," he said. Stanley, the little man, nodded his head and drank. Harry's eyes twinkled.

Nine

Inside the home dressing room, Ben was talking to the team. He was uneasy, his father hadn't been near them for over an hour, he had disappeared after the opening of the club. Bomber was coughing, the smell of the new paint irritated him, and Soggy kept thumping him on the back and fetching paper cups of water from the drinking tap. Soggy was very proud of the bath area, he spent hours in the showers, mumbling commentaries about his play to himself. The rest of the team was giving Ben full attention.

"Now listen you lot, just because we are down to ten men doesn't mean we go out there to lose, right? Let's give my Dad something back, he's sweated blood for you lot. We'll just have to run our legs off, cover everything. Dolly, you'll have to cover a lot of ground."

Mark stood up. "We could play for a draw."

"Rubbish," said Ben. "You get nothing like that. We'll go out to win! We had them rocking last time we played, we *let* them get that goal, remember?"

Nicky raised his head. "Ah, yes," he said, "but they'll have seen us play now. They know where we're strongest, who to mark."

Ben flushed with anger. "We can still beat them" – with his temper up Ben looked just like his father – "if we work hard and push it about. We've got to let them do all the running, no bad passes, yes?"

By now Soggy was lying full length on a changing bench. He sat up suddenly and asked: "Where is your Dad, Ben?"

"Soggy!" he roared. "For once in your life listen to what we are going to do."

Soggy sank back on the bench, quite put out by this new, fierce Ben. "OK, Ben, OK," said Soggy.

Ben glared at him, then went on: "We know they are suspect to crosses from either wing. Their goalie doesn't like high balls and he can't stop them too well on the ground either, so let's keep knocking the ball over into the middle and Nicky and I will hammer it on the ground."

Soggy sat up again. "Daisy cutters," he said loudly.

"Yes, Soggy," said Ben, "daisy cutters."

Soggy risked another observation. "He panics, you know, that goalie, if you run straight at him, he's chicken."

Ben put his hand up, "Soggy!" he said. "You stay back in defence, right?"

Soggy dropped his head. "Oh," he said softly.

"Defence!" repeated Ben. "Right?"

Soggy didn't like it, but he mumbled, "Right, Ben, right."

"*And* you Niggle," went on Ben, "And *you* Bomber, the only one I want to go on a run is Dolly, right? When he gets the ball, we know he's going through and we go with him, right?"

"Except me," intoned Soggy, in a very low voice.

Ben nodded his head up and down. "Except you Soggy."

"Right Ben, right."

"Right!" said Ben, warningly.

"Where *is* your Dad, Ben?" asked Soggy again.

"I don't know!" shouted Ben. "He went off with Jacky. Why don't you listen to what's being said, instead of asking stupid questions all the time?"

"I always ask stupid questions," said Soggy. Everybody laughed and the tension was lowered slightly.

Niggle took his sweater off. "Shouldn't we be getting changed?" he asked.

Ben looked at his watch. "Yes, OK," he muttered.

"Harry's not here either," interrupted Soggy, in a loud voice. They all looked about them.

"Yes," said Nicky, "where is everybody?"

"They've all deserted the sinking ship," replied Dolly.

"Nonsense," added Mark, "*my* Dad's here."

Soggy used his loud voice again. "He's no good on tactics, though, is he?"

"I've told you the tactics," Ben said coldly.

"I'm in defence?" asked Soggy.

Ben nodded, tight-lipped. "You're in defence," he agreed.

"Right," said Soggy.

"No solo runs, Soggy!" warned Ben.

"No solo runs," repeated Soggy.

"He's got it," shouted Nicky. "It's sunk in at long last." The boys gave Soggy a round of applause and he bowed to them.

The ten-man team started to change. Sweaters were pulled over heads, track shoes were kicked off, trousers thrown on the floor. Suddenly the door opened and Mr Dyker stood there with Jacky. A great moan of protest went up from the lads as they held jerseys, towels, anything they could lay their hands on, in front of them.

"Watch it!" came Bomber's muffled shout, caught with his pants off and his shirt over his head.

"It's changing time," shouted Adrian, going a very deep scarlet. The boys retreated as Mr Dyker pushed Jacky further into the room and closed the door. Dolly, who hadn't got anything on, hid behind the shower curtain. The rest of the team jostled each other, huddling together at the far end of the dressing room and silence descended.

"Jacky," said Soggy. "I think the team want you to wait outside while they change."

Mr Dyker smiled and held his hand up. "Just a minute Sogg," he said.

"Right, Mr Dyker," replied Soggy.

"Where've you been, Dad?" asked Ben.

Mr Dyker looked about the room. "Sizing up a new player," he said.

"Who?" asked Ben. "You can't just play anybody, Dad. They have to be signed on at the beginning of the season."

Mr Dyker smiled, "He is," he said.

"Who is it?" asked Mark.

"Can't be anyone I know," said Soggy. "I've seen all the names, all the registered ones anyway."

Mr Dyker rubbed his hands together. "It's true you have to register all your players at the beginning of the season," he said. "And this one is."

"I give up," said Nicky.

"Think!" said Mr Dyker.

"While we're thinking," said Nicky, "can Jacky wait outside, while we finish undressing?"

"No!" said Mr Dyker.

"What Dad?" said Ben.

"No!" repeated Mr Dyker.

"I don't understand," said Nicky.

Jacky turned her back on the boys and shut her eyes. They threw their coverings away and quickly pulled on team jerseys and shorts. Mr Dyker pointed to Jacky and then waved his finger at the boys. "That's the only time she'll have her eyes shut and her back turned towards you! She's your new left winger, so look after her."

The boys' mouths dropped open. Soggy dropped his shorts. Ben began to understand. "Is Jacky signed on, Dad?" he asked.

Mr Dyker nodded, a huge grin right across his face. "And her fees are paid."

"But she's a girl!" said Soggy.

Ben's eyes lit up. "She's a better player than you, Soggy."

"What happens if they find out?" asked Mark.

"They won't," said Mr Dyker. "And even if they do, there is nothing in the rules to say a girl cannot play in a football match, absolutely nothing."

"She always comes to training," said Ben, excited. "She knows all our moves."

Soggy added, "She's got a smashing shot and all."

Mr Dyker clapped his hands together. "Come on you lot, get changed, we've got a match to win."

Dolly stuck his head round the shower door. "Can someone throw me my shorts?" he asked in a strangled voice.

Jacky's shoulders began to shake, he was in her eyeline, but her eyes were tight shut. Ben threw Dolly his shorts and the others finished changing quickly, keeping an eye on Jacky. She made them all jump. "Can I turn round yet?" she asked.

"Yes," said Ben. "Come on, our flash winger, join the club."

Jacky shyly turned and faced the boys. Soggy was worried. "What on earth are you going to do when we all get in the showers, Jacky?" he said.

Nicky rescued her. "We won't have to use the showers this week, will we?"

"But they're brand new," said Soggy. "We haven't used them properly yet."

"Another week won't hurt," said Mark.

"Shall I get changed now, Mr Dyker?" Jacky's question hung in the air. The boys were quiet for a while, then they all started to shout, "Yeah!" "Why not?" "Go on!" "You're always watching us." "Come on Jacky, now you know what it feels like." The boys all stood in a group round Jacky and stared at her. Mr Dyker handed her a pair of boots and she placed them on the bench beside her. The boys started to whistle at her, Jacky smiled. They clapped their hands and Jacky began to peel her sweater off. It was too much for Soggy. "Eh, Jacky," he shouted, "our Mam will go mad!"

The sweater came off to reveal a number eleven jersey underneath. The boys all booed. Jacky grinned and pulled her jeans off, showing the football shorts underneath. She hung the jeans on a hook, "Satisfied, Nicky Brown?" she said.

"Why pick on me?" asked Nicky.

Jacky sat on the bench and began to lace up her boots, grinning at the team. "It's no good," said Soggy. "She looks like a girl."

Mr Dyker agreed with him. "He's right, Jacky. It's your hair. It's a dead giveaway."

Jacky paused, her head bent over her boots. "Cut it then," she said. "Cut it with the scissors in the first-aid bag."

Soggy's eyes lit up, "I'll do it," he said.

Mr Dyker grabbed him. "I'll do it," he said.

Ben looked at Jacky. "I'll lace your boots up," he said. She smiled at him.

 Back in the Plough, old Harry was getting into his stride. He sat at a little table in the corner watching Stanley negotiate the Saturday lunchtime crush with two foaming pints in each hand. Stanley plonked them down on the table top. Harry nodded at him. "Did you get the crisps?"

Stanley pulled two packets out of his overcoat pockets. "Cheese and onion?" demanded Harry.

Stanley nodded, "Cheese and onion," he repeated, and sat down.

Harry bit the corner off the packet and proceeded to flick the crisps into his mouth, watching Stanley all the time. Stanley took a long drink from his glass, licked his lips, nodded and turned to Harry. "I've got a confession to make," he said.

Harry looked at him. "So have I."

Stanley took another sip. "Shall I tell you mine first?" he asked. "Go on."

90

Stanley took another drink, wiped his mouth with the back of his hand, popped a crisp in his mouth, then started to search for the little salt bag. Harry gave him his. "Go on," said Harry again.

Stanley leant back in his chair. "I'm not from the council or anything, I'm just a debt collector. That notice I put up is not worth the paper it's printed on."

Harry watched him and crunched away on his crisps. "I know," he said blandly.

"You know?" said Stanley amazed.

"Aye," said Harry. "Shall I tell you my little confession?"

"Aye," said Stanley. "I think you better had."

"I've no money in the Building Society," said Harry, proudly.

"Haven't you?"

"Not a bean," said Harry, very loudly.

Stanley looked about him, very put out. "Then how are you going to pay me?" he asked.

Harry rubbed his hands together and sipped his pint. "I'm not, am I?" he said, banging the glass down on the table.

Stanley looked at him in amazement. "You're a crafty devil!"

"So are you," answered Harry, his eyes twinkling away. "It's my turn to get them, isn't it?"

Stanley shook his head. "You crafty old devil."

Harry rose and fought his way to the bar. "Make way, make way, man in a hurry," he shouted. The other customers, good naturedly, let him through to the bar and he turned and leant on it, looking back at Stanley, still shaking his head.

"Same again?" asked the barman.

Harry nodded. "Same again," he repeated, and started to whistle. He turned to a friendly fat man, standing at the bar. "We're playing in our first Cup game today, you know."

"Oh, aye," said the man. "Who might you be then?"

"Brenton boys, mate, Brenton boys, modelled on Everton – the best team ever to tread Wembley."

"Good luck then," the man said.

Harry nodded his thanks. "We'll need all of that," he said, and turned to get his beer.

Outside the palatial new clubhouse, the crowd was pushing and shoving to form a space for the two teams to walk out onto the pitch. It consisted mostly of the diehard supporters of Brenton. A loud cheer went up from the front. A lot of little boys jumped up and down, as they spotted the two teams coming out. Mark was in front with the rival captain leading Denton. Nicky was behind Mark, then Bomber and Wayne, then the rest. They pushed and shoved their way onto the pitch, as the crowd applauded them. The boys ran about warming up, and so far Jacky had not attracted any attention.

Mr Dyker came on the pitch with his team, giving them last-minute instructions. He told Mark to keep the sun at his back if he won the toss. Soggy was entertaining the crowd with a spot of high kicking, to loosen up his thigh muscles. He'd seen Kevin Keegan doing it once or twice, and he fancied his chances. There seemed a great danger of his leg flying right off into the crowd because of the effort he was putting in. He fixed a nearby Denton player with his evil eye, hoping to distract him. The lad just sniffed. The referee and his officials came on to the pitch and inspected the goal areas and corner flags. The pitch was in magnificent condition. The ball was placed on the centre spot and the crowd buzzed. On the trainers' bench, Mr Dyker turned to Mr Robson. "We're going to win," he said.

Mr Robson ignored him, he was busy counting the Brenton players. "Eight, nine, ten, eleven, that's twice I've counted," he said, "and each time I get eleven. You've got eleven men."

"We haven't," said Mr Dyker.

"You have," said Mr Robson, starting to count again.

Mr Dyker shook his head and grinned. "We've got ten men and a smashing little girl. Take another look at number eleven."

Mr Robson took a long look at Jacky as she ran about, trying to look anonymous. "Good lord," he said. "Is that allowed?"

Mr Dyker rubbed the back of his neck. He always got a dull pain there just before a match. "I've read the rule book four times, we are in order."

"Can she play?" asked Mr Robson.

"Like a dream."

"What if she gets knocked about?"

Mr Dyker looked at him. "Our lads will kill the offender," he said.

"Good lord," said Mr Robson, again. He mopped his face with his handkerchief and sat up on the bench very straight. "This is certainly going to be some match, then!"

"I hope so," said Mr Dyker.

On the field, Ben was talking to the rest of the players. "OK," he said, "this is where we take them apart, right? No going easy like last time!"

"Right," said Nicky.

"Right," echoed Mark.

"Soggy?" shouted Ben.

"I know," said Soggy. "Defence!"

Ben wagged his finger at him. "Don't forget."

Soggy nodded glumly.

Ben looked across to his left. "All right, Jack?" he shouted, grinning.

Jacky shuffled about with embarrassment and waved she was OK. She didn't trust her gruff voice just yet.

Denton had won the toss and were looking very confident, tough and polished in their lovely kit. The thin referee with spindly legs and a beaky nose was satisfied the spectacle was ready to begin. He checked his two watches, nodded in turn to his two linesmen, and with a very elaborate gesture, blew his whistle and this Cup match was on.

Denton kicked off. Their number nine went forward with the ball, he dummied past Bomber, but Niggle was in like a terrier and won the ball. He played it back to Soggy, who collected it and moved to his right. A Denton forward came rushing at him, Soggy swerved past him. Oh what a lovely dummy, Soggy said to himself! What a class player we have here! He's a mover, he's a groover! Soggy looked up and spotted Jacky moving well. He flashed the ball to her. She collected it without pausing and raced down the touchline with it, a defender racing with her. Suddenly Jacky stopped dead and trod on the ball, the defender went hurtling on. She smiled and delicately chipped the ball to Ben in the middle, who chested it down and turned with it. He struck the ball as it hit the ground and it came off his foot like a thunderbolt. The back of the net rippled and bulged and the Denton goalkeeper stood there with his mouth open. The crowd loved it, they went mad, cheering, chanting, applauding. In the excitement, Jacky rushed to Ben, threw her arms around him, and kissed him without thinking. They both realised what they were doing at the same time, and broke away sheepishly. Ben blushed. The team behind them shouted, "Wha-hay!" Nicky was close to Jacky. "You won't do that to me if I score, will you?" he shouted.

"You shut up, Nicky Brown," shouted Jacky, but she was laughing.

Brenton ran back for the centre. The Denton team were not looking too cocky now. One down in the first few minutes, this was unthinkable! They kicked off and pressed towards the Brenton goal. Adrian robbed their number eight with a crunching tackle and pushed the ball to Nicky. He pivoted with it, his long hair swishing round his face. He dummied left then right and the Denton midfield player was lost, and Nicky was free and striding down the right wing. He cut in sharply and lost another defender. Two more were coming at him. He slipped the ball to Ben at the last moment, having drawn the two defenders beautifully. Ben caught a flash of a running Brenton jersey to his left. He pushed the ball into the player's path, it was Jacky, running like a gold medallist. She clouted the ball very hard, it whistled past the bemused Denton keeper for another smashing goal. Ben ran to Jacky and was about to throw his arm round her, when they both remembered and shook hands instead.

Half-way down the pitch, Denton's manager and trainer, Noel and Ronnie, were having a terrible match. As they watched the Denton players walking back to the kick off again, they were almost numb with shock. "Amazing!" said Noel. "That winger who just scored is a reserve player, Ronnie, did you know?"

"I wish they'd left him there," said Ronnie, and started to shout to the sick-looking Denton players. "Come on chaps, get stuck in! Let's see some effort, come on!"

"Yes," chanted Noel. "Effort, chaps, effort, come on – let's have a goal."

The game started again and the play moved up and down, with Brenton pushing the ball to each other like world beaters.

By now Harry had swayed into the ground with Stanley, and taken up a favourable position on the touchline. He turned to Stanley, "Best bloody team you'll ever see, Stanley," he shouted, above the roars.

"I'm impressed," said Stanley, smiling, and he tried to get his briefcase back, but Harry wouldn't let it go, he clutched it to his chest.

94

Jacky ran past Harry and off the pitch to retrieve the ball. She prepared to throw it in. "Eh, number eleven," shouted Harry. "Any score yet?"

"Two nil to us," shouted Jacky, and threw the ball to Ben.

"Great, great," said Harry. "Did you hear that," he shouted to Stanley. "Two nil to us, we had to let them win last time, you know."

"Oh, yes?" said Stanley, not quite with it.

Harry's face was puzzled, as the problem in his mind got bigger and bigger. He tried to focus on the fast-disappearing Brenton players, as they pushed towards the other goal, but his eyes started to water again. Well I'm blowed, he said to himself, am I seeing things? I could have sworn that was little Jacky in a number eleven shirt, taking that throw in. She spoke to me, I'm sure she did. What's going on? He looked about him, disbelief and confusion written on his face. He looked at his feet. I've lost my bloody dog and all! I'm in a right state, he mumbled to himself.

Most of the supporters were watching the Brenton lads' destruction of the other team, with exquisite pleasure. Stan Baker, puffing away on his new pipe, nodded sagely at each piece of skill as it was presented, cheering every attempt at a goal, every touch of the ball. He removed his pipe and used it as a pointer. "Look at that lads, look at that skill! Makes it all worth it, doesn't it – eh?" The others nodded agreement.

Mr Woodgate added: "There'll be no holding this team now. They'll pick everything up. They'll hammer everyone in the League. They'll take the Cup and the League table, I'm telling you."

"That'll mean Germany next year," shouted Adrian's father. "We'll have to organise a party, what do you say?"

Mr Baker gestured again at the match. "The way those kids are playing, anything is possible."

Mr Dyker had seen Harry and Stanley arrive and take up their positions on the touchline. He smiled to himself as he saw Harry looking about for Bob. He realised that Harry had kept Stanley out of the boys' hair until the kick off. Neither of them wanted the boys worrying about debts and strangers, certainly not on a Cup day. Mr Dyker made his way over and put his arm round Harry's shoulders. "Hello, Harry," he said quietly.

"Hello, boss," replied Harry, with surprise and relief. Mr Dyker looked at Harry's kind, weatherbeaten face, a bit flushed now. "We're winning Harry," he said.

"Are we boss?" said Harry, his eyes glistening.

Mr Dyker gave Harry a long hug and straightened his tie for him. "Yes, Harry," he repeated quietly. "We're winning!"

Mr Dyker felt good, it's all going to work, he thought. We've won, we've beaten our luck at last – it's going to work. A loud cheer went up, Mark had put away another goal for Brenton. The team came running back as he had drilled into them. Make the other team wonder where you get your energy from, he had told them. He caught sight of Ben and waved. Ben opened his arms wide, as if to say, why were we worried this morning? Mr Dyker grinned and flicked his right hand at Ben. The game started again. He turned and considered the new clubhouse behind him. Those rafters will ring tonight, he thought. But something disturbed him, something was wrong, and he couldn't quite put his finger on it. He checked the positions of all his players. They were spot on. Slowly, he realised what it was. The dull ache in his leg had stopped. He stamped on it, grinned happily, waved at Ben and, like a good manager, planned the next match.